The Honor of the Tribe

ALSO BY RACHID MIMOUNI:

Une peine à vivre (novel), 1991
Le Printemps n'en sera que plus beau (novel)
Le Fleuve détourné (novel), 1982
Tombéza (novel), 1989
La Ceinture de l'ogresse (short stories), 1990

Rachid Mimouni

THE HONOR OF
THE TRIBE

A NOVEL

TRANSLATED FROM THE FRENCH

BY JOACHIM NEUGROSCHEL

William Morrow and Company, Inc. · New York

It is the policy of William Morrow and Company, Inc., and its imprints and
affiliates, recognizing the importance of preserving what has been written, to print
the books we publish on acid-free paper, and we exert our best efforts to that end.

Library of Congress Cataloging-in-Publication Data
Mimouni, Rachid.
[Honneur de la tribu. English]
The honor of the tribe / by Rachid Mimouni;
translated from the French by Joachim Neugroschel.
p.   cm.
Translation of: L'honneur de la tribu.
ISBN 0-688-09746-4
I. Title.
PQ3989.2.M494H6613   1992
843—dc20   91-45161   CIP

Printed in the United States of America

First Edition

1 2 3 4 5 6 7 8 9 10

BOOK DESIGN BY DOROTHY S. BAKER

All stories deepen into fables.

PAUL VALÉRY

This is the Mother of humans for this so young
Husband in her arms—he, instructed to begin
Here and not at the place from which they were driven.

PIERRE EMMANUEL

The Honor of the Tribe

"YOU HAVE TO KNOW that the Revolution has not forgotten you," he declared upon his arrival.

We had no inkling of what lay ahead for us.

But I can't begin this story without evoking the name of the Almighty, the All-Knowing, the Creator of all creatures, the Ruler of all events, and the Master of all destinies. He has set down everything in the Great Book of the World.

Thus, it is His approval that I seek for my story. Since this is no fairy tale, I do not have to wait until nightfall lest our children be born bald. You will listen to me without grasping what I say. Our tongue has fallen into disuse, and it is spoken by only a few survivors among us. It will perish with us. Our past will thus be swallowed up, as will the memory of the fathers of our fathers. No one will know what the lives of the inhabitants of this village were like for over a century and a half.

So let your machine be imbued with my words.

Today we are abandoned on the shore of the raging river which you believe will take you to a snug harbor.

We know that if the tree is to regain its vigor for a new springtime, all we have to do is prune off a few branches.

We accept this.

But you will be swindled.

And when you realize that you have to go back upstream to rediscover that essential but subtle part of yourselves, you will unearth those old tapes that will resurrect our voices. However, in order to find us, you must first learn to decipher our idiom.

We will await you at the end of your suffering.

So start spinning your machine.

It all began during a July whose Dog Days were such a terrible affliction that they eventually broke down both man and beast. Our idle oldsters spent their days slipping from shadow to shadow, trying to elude sunbeams crueler than stings of wasps. The heat plunged them into a state of utter indolence, robbing them of the strength to keep up their chitchat; a faint nod of the head was their sole response to the terse greeting of the latest person to join them. Our reputedly dynamic women no longer dared to venture out into the courtyards of their houses, which had become more sweltering than a threshing floor; they drained their weariness in lackadaisical gestures that aroused our fancies. The children, the children themselves, all the children, who were usually more feverish than ants at harvest time, preferred taking refuge under the huge eucalyptuses. We assumed that our teenagers were slaving away in the fields, for among us, an honorable head of family must stop working once his firstborn male is old enough to replace him. But actually, our teenagers were tranquilly snoozing under the olive trees, awoken only by the bite of the sun and then crawling over to the shifted shadow. Even the flies had stopped pestering the living; they were probably dozing in some merciful haven.

It must have been noon, and the village looked as if it had turned into stone.

It was then that we spied the agitated silhouette of Ali son of Ali, our mailman, at the farthest turning of the single lane that capriciously dissected our straggly hamlet. He was hurrying toward the square of three fig trees, under which the elders of the djemaa (assembly) were lying. We were intrigued by his unusually jittery haste, for we had always regarded the son of Ali as a sensible and reasonable man, who knew how to behave in all circumstances, particularly since his respectability was reinforced by his status of civil servant, which assured him a regular monthly salary, summer or winter, rain or snow, or even when the heat was crumpling up our customary landscape.

Georgeaud, who had abandoned his fly-filled grocery shop for a less oppressive atmosphere, edged his torso up by propping himself on one elbow.

"What could have gotten into that fine son of Ali?"

His question piqued the curiosity of several turbans, and they consented to rise several inches in order to observe the approach of the man of letters.

A sagacious analyst of human passions, Georgeaud, contemplating the incongruous excitement of the uniform-wearer, learnedly concluded:

"This can mean only one thing: he must have received a favorable answer to his application."

"What are you talking about?"

The fresh-air fiends dreaded any event that might break the humdrum but comforting succession of identical days that stealthily lapped up their lives. All of them had been born and bred in this village, seeing and greeting one another every morning and evening. All of them were promptly notified about the slightest incident. Everybody was acquainted with every last detail of every other life, including mine, just as everybody could reel off a detailed profile, without mistakes or omissions, of the son of Ali, run down a complete list of his wife's kith and kin, give the ages of his children, specify the exact year that he had assumed his position, and describe his daily schedule.

We all knew that every day at nine A.M. the mailman entered his office—the small room adjoining the municipal annex. This sufficed to distinguish him from all the other inhabitants of the village, for he was the only one to enjoy the privilege of not rising till after the sun, whether the days grew longer or shorter. He would spend half an hour in that room, waiting for possible customers. His hopes were regularly dashed, for the only letters on which he noisily whacked his stamp were the ones that he himself had written for senders who didn't know the Roumi alphabet. These brief missives were generally nothing more than money-order requests to a son who had emigrated to France, a country where the living was said to be easier but so much more anguished. Georgeaud could attest to this, having spent twenty years in Paris.

"It's the land of frenzy."

Georgeaud hadn't had the foggiest notion of what was happening to him from the day that two gendarmes came to flank him and lead him away in handcuffs to the regroupment center (while the son of the Caid of Sidi Bounemeur, whom he had dared to defy, was sniggering behind his back) until the day when Georgeaud had found himself discharged, handed some old civilian togs, and left penniless in the immense city, which sprawled indecently across the plain like a satiated paramour across her bed, and which was fed by a procession of barges hauled along a flabby inland river that delighted in endlessly meandering to and fro as if fearing its demise in the ocean, where all waters intermingle. Georgeaud was lost amid those overly broad streets, where the vast store windows brazenly flaunted all their contents as if to tempt customers, where the streetlights shone all night long, where blaring automobiles drove in sheer anarchy, where the women, as numerous as the men, strolled around, unabashed and unembarrassed, protected only by a small fine veil that made a derisive effort to conceal the upper parts of their faces, or else they sat on café terraces, simpering as they reaped admiration and compliments. Georgeaud admitted to us that he had been fascinated by the local virtues of ambition and patience: the inhabitants dared to construct buildings so solid that they would outlive all time, so enormous that these men knew they couldn't complete them during their own lives; they were busy digging underground galleries so vast that whole trains could pass through with all their cars, following and crossing one another nonstop, diving into the river but never getting wet. Georgeaud told us that they had manufactured such enormous quantities of iron and steel that they moved through a purely metallic universe.

"What made the biggest impact on you in that land of frenzy?" we would ask him.

"Lots of things."

"But what more than anything else?"

"The water."

"The water?"

"Yes."

"That's all?"

"Yes, there was water everywhere, a liquid abundance, a profusion of water—lakes, ponds, pools, fountains, and even more often: streams and rivers, side by side, separating and rejoining, and so wide that heavy ships sail upstream and down, passing and greeting one another with siren blasts. And all those canals with bridges that rise or pivot to let the barges go through, and all those mysterious mechanisms—more intricate than the most intricate sura of the Koran—that lift them or drop them, like magic. I was shocked to see that all this water flowed indolently into the ocean, and no one cared. One billionth of that mass could moisten our arid gravel fields! Drink, oh my crackled earth, may your wounds heal, and may we get back the happy valley and the verdure that calms the soul. May our breasts swell up at last!"

All that Georgeaud retained of his forced military escapade was the memory of confused tramping, indescribable disorder, a series of wanderings from bivouac to bivouac, center to center, barracks to barracks, a succession of waiting periods, packs on, arms at the order, a cacophony of commands and countercommands. The expected trucks were several days late. The junior officers began hectoring the draftees in order to speed up the embarkment, as if the outcome of the war depended on their speediness. But once the trucks were finally loaded, they refused to get going, and after a long, patient wait, the soldiers jumped to the ground and resumed their march as they watched the heavy but now-empty trucks charge off in the same direction. The rustic station, which was beleaguered at night, eventually welcomed a train that was chockablock with down-and-out buck privates, who were told to climb down, then climb out, then climb down again. During idle moments in their multiple quarterings, the officers trained them to march in step, recommending a robotlike rigidity. After endless mishaps, the contingents wound up in the port, where the huge ship was waiting for them in her bovine placidity. She consented to admit the interminable parade of conscripts into her huge belly. As she started pitching, panic spread through the herd of shaved heads confined in the hold. The draftees had fearfully watched the shore moving away and they were terrified at the thought of their immense coffin sinking into the waves. Most of them released the contents of their innards, and those who, fleeing the nauseating miasmas, had the courage to go up on deck were petrified by the spectacle of the vast expanse of water surrounding them. They expected to see ocean monsters looming from the surface, the creatures of ancestral tales about the voyages of their ancient forebears, who had been foolhardy enough to venture out into the most perilous seas. However, their timorous descendants were wise enough to realize that it was useless roaming the world in order to discover its unknown lands, and even more useless studying them in order to explore the hidden and implacable laws governing them. That arrogant craving for knowledge competed heretically with divine omniscience. So the progeny decided to stop confronting the mysteries of unexplored countries and they agreed to close those profane tomes and lock them away in arcane and inaccessible places. Rejecting the quests and torments of inquiry, they lived in the comfort of the certitudes of their faith. And now, hundreds of years later, their sons found themselves in boots and helmets, sailing across those forgotten seas, being led against their will toward a thoroughly unknown destiny.

After docking, the ship disgorged a series of flabby and spineless bodies. It took them several days to recover their taste for food and stable ground under their feet. Then the harassing marches and the repeated waiting periods recommenced, the whimsical trains, the trucks bogging down in several feet of mud. Next, the regiments passed through a succession of villages drowsing in such pregnant grayness as to discourage all smiles and hopes. They camped on a hilltop, dug ditches, set up casemates, and ensconced themselves underground.

"I saw nothing," Georgeaud told us. "If it hadn't been for the cannon booming over our heads, you'd've thought we'd been asked to play hide and go-seek."

After the victory, the French began rebuilding their devastated country, and so Georgeaud easily found work in a construction firm—Georgeaud and Son, where he started as an unskilled laborer, hauling wheelbarrow after wheelbarrow of endless loads of cement, through snow and cold that turned his fingers stiffer than vine-shoots after the dressing.

"Let me tell you in all confidence: throughout those twenty years, I never groveled. I learned their lifestyle. I drank their grape wine and ate their pork, I shaved off my moustache and fornicated with their women. God forgive me. I forgot all about the very existence of our village. Exile laminates your life more heavily than their monstrous road rollers."

"What did they think of you?" we asked him.

"They learned to hate us because we were poor and badly off, they made fun of us because we didn't know how to run their machines, they despised us because we didn't like their products or their cooking."

Since he had never gotten in touch with us, we thought he was lying in the soil of infidels after being killed in the dreadful turmoil that had driven the most powerful nations on the planet to slaughter one another savagely. But one day, without warning, he stepped out of a taxi loaded with valises full of the most bizarre objects: an apparatus that congealed images on paper—in the teeth of the Prophet's beard—copper wires that captured distant voices which all of us could hear, a lamp that shone without a flame. However, his mind was even more encumbered with wacky ideas, as we realized later on.

Thus, he acted scandalized upon noting that the village had neither running water nor electricity.

"Running water?"

"Yes, in your own house. You turn a faucet, and there's a mysterious surge, and a furious stream spurts out, it's more powerful than the pearly liquid of an adolescent penetrating his first woman."

"In our well, we've got singing mineral water, it's more joyful than a virgin on her wedding day."

"What about electricity?"

"What good is it?"

"It can light the streets and run appliances in the home."

"What streets? What appliances?"

Much to our good fortune, Georgeaud's diabolical gadgets quickly collapsed, so they no longer troubled the minds of our greedy youths. But the things that had been put inside his skull proved more resistant. That was why, from the very outset, he had encouraged the son of Ali to file his application, then supported his numerous follow-up letters.

We continued to like the son of Ali, despite his ambivalence. We believed that the community had lost the child that he had been when his crazy father decided to have him brought up by an uncle who had taken refuge in Sidi Bounemeur after some shady moral incident. Ali's father insisted that the boy attend the foreign school, as if it were not enough for a son of Islam to be taught by our sheik, who, after all, had perfectly mastered every single sura in the Holy Book, from the first to the last. But Ali's father had always cultivated eccentricity, which, for us, is the worst of vices. After several years, the schoolboy came back to us, but not, we felt, in spirit. Actually, it was only much later that we realized they had planted the shifty and ravaging seeds of modernity in his mind.

"What's it all about?" the imam repeated after checking his watch and noting with delight that he still had an hour of loafing before it was time for prayers.

"It's about his application for a telephone," Georgeaud replied.

The interest of the onlookers fizzled out like air from a balloon.

For truth's sake, we have to admit that the populace of Zitouna didn't give a tinker's damn about that vague business of a telephone line. They felt more than lucky that they could send and get the trickle of correspondence handled by Ali son of Ali: every morning at nine-thirty on the dot, he would straddle his bike and peddle three miles to the highway in order to remit the mail to or receive it from the driver of the bus that linked Sidi Bounemeur to the cities of the plain. All that Ali had to do, upon returning to Zitouna, was to station himself on the fig-tree square and distribute the letters. Next, as was his wont, he would thrash out his modernization projects with Georgeaud, who approved or condemned on the basis of his years of experience in foreign countries. The grocer never let the postman leave without exhorting him.

"Don't be discouraged by the indifference of these dinosaurs. They've lost all hope for the future and they're on the verge of doubting their past."

Ali son of Ali slowed down as he approached the fig-tree square. His armpits were haloed with big, moist stains and his crimson face was drenched with sweat. Doffing his cap, he exclaimed, "Have you heard the news?"

A pointless question. A long time ago, the villagers had assigned him the task, over and above his official function, of informing them as briefly as possible about the events harrying the world; for he was the only one who read the newspaper that the bus driver brought him along with the mail.

"They're installing the telephone?" asked Georgeaud.

"No, it's a lot more important."

"A new war?"

Barely one year after his impromptu return to Zitouna, Georgeaud had experienced the worst terror of his life upon learning that the frenzied countries had gone back to tearing each other's guts out.

"Are they trying to exterminate us?"

Afraid of being called up again, Georgeaud fled Zitouna, taking refuge in the city, at the home of a fellow conscript who had fought in the same campaigns.

"Do you think they're gonna draft us again?" They asked each other in chorus.

They calmed one another's fears, citing their age and the sacrifices they had already made.

"The Roumis are fair-minded. They're going to choose new victims for their new war."

Georgeaud resurfaced in Zitouna several months later.

"Did the Caïd's men come looking for me?"

We put his mind at ease.

"A new war?" Georgeaud exclaimed insistently.

"No, it's something completely different. Zitouna is being made the district seat!"

"I CAN TELL YOU I'm not coming empty-handed," he declared upon his arrival.

The topic that had so greatly excited the son of Ali failed to pull the refugees on the fig-tree square out of their feckless indifference—except for Mohamed, who instantly took the postman aside to ask for an explanation.

"Does this mean we'll no longer be under the administration of Sidi Bounemeur?"

Our hamlet had always been territorially attached to the neighboring village. During the colonial era, the wise administrator of the joint parish, satisfied that we were paying our taxes regularly, never tried to meddle in our affairs, and so we continued enjoying the rare privilege of being left to our own devices. But, a few months after independence, we were notified from a distant place that henceforth we would have to exercise our brand-new and hard-won sovereignty by holding elections and voting for a mayor and a town council, who would be in charge of public matters . . . in Sidi Bounemeur. Since we were invited to present candidates, we unanimously designated our compatriot Mohamed.

Starting in his teens, Mohamed had shown a strange attraction to politics—in defiance of our sages. When a cease-fire was announced between our maquis and France, Mohamed went to Sidi Bounemeur and, being certain that all danger was past for uniform-wearers, he joined the newly constituted corps of the local Forces. Several weeks later, he came back to Zitouna, swaggering about in his khaki and his kepi, which were identical with those worn by the soldiers we had fought. He was perfectly ridiculous. And we realized that this man must have very little dignity but loads of ambition if he had swapped the clothes of his fathers for this grotesque disguise. Since his skin was white and his eyes the color of water, the mountain-dwellers he ran into mistook him for a Roumi. Some of them contemplated cutting his throat. But luckily for him, he had a quick tongue, and the tardy avengers were surprised by their blunder upon recognizing our inimitable local accent. The apostate was peppered with the stinging comments of our oldsters, but we were astonished at the envy and admiration he aroused in our young men. Some of them even wanted to follow in his footsteps. The intransigence of their fathers managed to dissuade them.

We had been raised to worship fidelity, and we despised renegades. Mohamed's ancestors had been outlaws, banished from all places, and our tribe had been willing to take them in. After several generations, most of them had forgotten their own origins and thought they were the same as ours. But eventually, atavisms resurface. Our sages were right in advising us to observe prudence. Mohamed's new status made an impact on the girl he was courting and broke down her father's reluctance. The wedding took place after all, and, truth to tell, it was a happy marriage. Despite his cravings for success, Mohamed proved to be a good husband, then a good head of family.

Mohamed took off for his barracks a few days after the ceremony. But to our great surprise, he reappeared in our village within a couple of months, wearing mufti; he promptly set about stoking the fire in his father's café. It was only some time later that the son of Ali told us the reason for this unforeseen return to the old homestead. After the liberation, the leaders of the struggle against the foreign occupant were unable to limit their respective ambitions in a friendly way; so they decided to resort to a force of arms again. Some of them had the zany idea of drawing on that lastborn corps, which was composed of troops who believed they could benefit from the prestige of the maquis without ever firing a shot. A number of them deserted, including Mohamed.

Next, blatantly unfazed by his misadventure, Mohamed decided to join the Party, and he began traveling all the way to Sidi Bounemeur to attend the weekly cell meetings. Upon returning, he would try to get us interested in what had been debated, but no one paid him the slightest heed, not even Georgeaud, who sometimes had peculiar ideas resulting from his many years in France. Thus it was the café-owner's son who jubilantly announced the arrival of this delegation coming from so far away. With the help of several teenagers, he rigged up a small tribune for them. But since none of us owned any chairs, the zealot decided to smash down the door of the abandoned villa of Martial, the colonist. Mohamed's act of brigandage made us realize that his heart was swarming with the scorpions of ambition.

We slaughtered several goats in honor of these delegates. But we were outraged by their wretched manners and their lack of couth. They were in such a great hurry to reel off their speeches that they waved away the tea they were offered and they declined our invitation to share our evening couscous. Lacking an electric loudspeaker, they were forced to shout their heads off in the sun. We listened politely. After performing their thankless chore, they precipitously jumped back into their cars, which were ocher from the dust of the road, and they disappeared without so much as waving.

We were deeply chagrined.

* * *

After their departure, we gathered round the imam and agreed to sacrifice Mohamed's military ardor on the altar of community peace.

"This way we'll have designated a candidate, and they'll leave us alone. In any case, the boy is dying to be elected."

Benefiting from our unanimous vote, Mohamed became town councilor. The shrewd mayor of Sidi Bounemeur, who absolutely refused to be saddled with problems of tribal rivalries, appointed him his deputy in charge of the administration of Zitouna. So we had our peace, and Mohamed now strutted about with a seal and a fountain pen in his pocket, signing and stamping whenever, wherever, and whatever he was asked to sign and stamp. Everything went very smoothly, our representative acted as a bulwark against the caprices of the authorities and their attempts at meddling. We had to admit that he proved to be perfect in exercising his new function, acquitting himself quite efficiently of his expected role. Thus, we were not long in restoring him to favor and, when his father died, we admitted Mohamed into the djemaa despite his position and his youth.

The most notable incident occurred with the arrival of the pseudoforeigner. We were not in the habit of receiving foreigners. The only ones we'd known were a couple of eccentric oldsters who mistook us for bees and came to study our manners and mores. These curious men spent whole days in the sun, watching us live our lives. Since they had been sent by the administration of the joint parish, we managed to ignore them despite our sense of hospitality. Then there was that trio of mint-tea lovers. They climbed out of a vehicle that looked like an American jeep, and all they had on was shorts and T-shirts, in which, they thought, they would suffer less from the blazing sun. There was the man with graying hair, the white, blond, ageless woman, and also the virgin, who behaved very wantonly, with all the allurement of her generous adolescence. They were overjoyed to be sitting on a mat in the café, taking their tea and lots of photos. They were even interested in our donkeys.

"That's odd," Georgeaud told us.

"What?"

"I recognize their speech. They're Germans. The people we fought and beat. I thought they were all dead."

However, this newcomer, like us, had a skin like ripe dates and carob-colored eyes, even though he refused to speak the vernacular. Our stupefaction reached its peak when the intruder announced that he was the teacher and that he had come to open a school.

"A school?"

"The mayor of Sidi Bounemeur has informed me that the former annex of the French military building could be used for this purpose."

Outraged, we had the most eloquent among us explain that we had not waited until his arrival to think about the education of our progeny and that since time immemorial the local male offspring had been placed under the aegis of the sheik, who was also the imam of our mosque; the boys would store up suras of the Revelation, one after another, and they could regurgitate them on demand, at an incredible speed, and with such a wonderful delivery that the verses banged and bumped, nearly shattering one another; and the most gifted of these lads sometimes even managed to memorize all sixty parts, that is, the totality of the divine tiding.

Our spokesman added, "Please don't be misled by the material destitution in which these tots live or by our seemingly off-handed attitude toward them. They are our liver, and we keep watch over them like the apples of our eyes. It is not simply the modesty of our means that prevents us from showering them with brilliant trinkets from the frenzied countries, as the wealthy do in the capital. You see, we set great store by raising our children in the rigor of austerity and the virtue of hard work, and we never forget to supply them with rules and moral precepts which will help them to live in true comfort."

The teacher went into detail: "I am talking about the government school."

Our interpreter explained to him that in any case, all of us, as true believers, regarded the contents of the Book as the sum total of all earthly knowledge and that consequently these sons of Islam had no need whatsoever to pervert their minds in places that excluded God and dispensed nothing but heresies.

Our contradictor proved obstinate.

"The law says that schooling is obligatory for all children."

The onlookers shrugged. The man was told that this forgotten place was as far from the capital as the earth from the sky. That our climate was very different. When a sky as imperturbably serene as the consciences of its inhabitants was announced for the city, our region was still coping with the rigors of a January that had borrowed a day from its successor in order to reduce us to a state of unconditional surrender. That the contrast between our village and the capital was a lot more anguishing. These laws that came from so far away lost their breath en route or else fell into decay long before reaching the slope that led to our area. Thus, all we inherited was dismal avatars of metropolitan whims, like that laughable obligation to put neon signs on our stores even though we were still lighting our homes with carbide or kerosene lamps.

Our town councilor felt it was high time he intervened.

"This foreigner is right all the same. According to the law, schooling is obligatory."

"That's true," confirmed Georgeaud, who was waiting for a precedent to challenge the consensus of the population. "In France, where, as you all know, I lived for a long time, the mayor even has the right to send recalcitrant parents to prison."

Mohamed, wavering, scratched his head.

He was trying to understand the opposition of the son of Ali, who was now threatened in his monopoly as sole speaker of the language of the Roumis.

He understood the imam's desperate eagerness to get rid of the teacher. His intrusion compromised the sheik's status as sole dispenser of knowledge.

Mohamed knew why the inhabitants were so reluctant. With the independence, and the departure of the soldiers occupying the French military annex, the villagers had debated and discussed the appropriation of the sheet-metal structure that had thus been liberated. They finally agreed to turn it into a community stable. As it happened, our religious leader owned the largest herd.

After a long hesitation, Mohamed addressed the disturber. "Needless to say, we will be happy to have our sons benefit from all the new knowledge that is copied from foreigners. However, this metal tent could not house your pupils. It is in no condition to do so, since the summer transforms it into a steam bath and the winter into an ice pit. We would have to build a real school, with brick walls and with cement to hold the bricks together. Tomorrow I'm going to ask the mayor of Sidi Bounemeur to grant the necessary funds."

The instructor was not hoodwinked by this stalling ploy. He left, threatening to go over our heads to the superior authorities. Our smiles informed him that the only superior we had was God, and that we didn't give a good goddamn about the opinions of those authorities. Naturally, we never heard from the instructor again, but our life was no longer business as usual. The intruder with the naive comments had strewn a few seeds that didn't take long to sprout in the minds of several inhabitants of Zitouna. Georgeaud, who owned no livestock whatsoever, was the first to rekindle the debate. His persistence won over the son of Ali, and the two of them actively campaigned for the establishment of a government school.

The mailman and the grocer extolled the advantages of a lay instruction adapted to the demands of modern times and enabling pupils to learn the language of the Roumis, which was the only thing giving access to regular jobs and salaries, both summer and winter, despite droughts, locust invasions, and the diseases that decimated the herds—all the more so, they perfidiously added, since schooling was totally free of charge.

The two campaigners were opposed by the imam's clan, who cited the numerous perils to which those defenseless young minds would be exposed. The sheik actually went so far as to hint that he would refuse to dispense the holy word to anyone who dared to set foot in that heretical institution.

The debates, although serene and temperate during the first few days, rapidly grew more and more acrimonious, which was bound to revive old grudges and reignite ancient conflicts. In the thick of the fray, we felt the wind of discord blasting over us and we remembered the words of the Jewish mountebank.

We then clearly realized the new danger brewing over our community. The wisest men now had to intervene in order to restore mutual understanding and cordiality. Mohamed was one of those sages.

The incident left us with the feeling that unhappiness always comes with foreigners.

Yes, our collective memory is tenacious. This is because our tribe has known so much misery. Let me tell you how our ancestors came to settle in Zitouna.

"YOUR FATE IS now in your hands," he added as he got out of the car.

Upon hearing the news, Georgeaud, who had left his grocery shop in the custody of the flies, silently went back in order to reflect at leisure. He took a fresh look at the poor shelves lined with the few products that could be sold to the local clientele. This examination moved him to pull a long, condescending face.

"We'll have to make some changes. Highly learned people are going to settle here. They'll be drawing huge regular salaries. I'll have to supply them with those so expensive and so profitable extras. I'll need to think about expanding. My cousin, the burnoose embroiderer, has a place, and I'm going to try and purchase it. His eyes are so worn out from working that he can't recognize his friends, much less the early signs of the coming upheavals. He'll trade me his shop for three goats. I'll be rich and I'll put in a telephone for the pleasure of saying hello to my old war buddies in France."

But Georgeaud was an eccentric, and his long exile had fostered his development of cranks and crotchets verging on heresy.

As for Mohamed, he wondered if he was to finally shake off the tutelage of Sidi Bounemeur and assume the position of full-fledged mayor.

"Are you sure?" he persisted.

"In fact, *they* are going to be dependent on *us*," the son of Ali affirmed.

"When is it going to happen?"

"It won't be long now."

For his part, the son of Ali, no longer doubting that his application would be granted, started dreaming about a real state-of-the-art central post office, with a row of numbered windows, a postage-canceling machine, and a switchboard endlessly buzzing with telephone calls.

All the other inhabitants of Zitouna, anxious about the announced changes, tried to bury their dim fears deep in their hearts.

"A prefect? What's that?" asked Djelloul the blacksmith.

"I've never met one," replied Aïssa the cripple.

"What's going to happen to us?"

Little did we know that our troubles were only just beginning.

Until then, we had lived in serenity, ignoring, and ignored by, the world, knowing how to benefit from the experiences of our sages and the instructions of our saints, translating them into laws and customs that were applied by an assembly whose members were appointed on the basis of their knowledge, their sense of justice, or their eloquence. We had learned how to bear up against the onslaughts of adversity, fully aware that the greatest dangers surged from our own midst.

It was over a century and a half ago that our ancestors had begun to understand and interpret the forewarnings of new times. They said, "The sons of Islam have been hibernating for a long time, in thrall to a dream of long-gone power. Each country reckoned with its neighbor's protective strength, from Baghdad to Cairo, from Cordoba to the

Sublime Porte. But under the blows of the Christians, Spain was reconquered province by province, and Granada was menaced. No one came to her rescue, despite her pleas for help. No sooner had the Castilian occupied the Alhambra than his ships harassed the fortifications of the Maghrebian harbors. The attackers were often defeated, but sometimes they managed to gain a foothold in certain ports. Now came the fearsome fleets of those nations who had become past masters in the art of melting down not only lead and copper, but also iron and the hardest metals. And we have awoken feeble and defenseless. We are vanquished, and utterly routed. Now our sole concern is to survive. Many lusters will wear by before we lift our heads again. If we manage to preserve peace and our unity, then perhaps the great-grandchildren of our great-grandchildren will regain enough hope, ambition, and vanity to peer into the future. But we ourselves are doomed. History carries grudges.

All this took place during the long retreat that was to lead the scattered ranks of our conquered tribe all the way to this area.

"How are we to survive in this land of desolation?" asked those of us who longed for the happy valley that had enchanted their youth. "All we see around us is dust and gravel. No spring and no river. No tree and no grass. Does it ever rain here? What silt will nourish the grain? What will our animals feed on? What swing plow will turn over this soil? Where is the black earth that opened under the plowshare like a loving woman to the first caress of her chosen man? The earth that, equally pregnant, rewarded you for your efforts, often in less time? Where are those lively, gurgling brooks heading—the ones that used to enjoy winding lazily through our orchards? Have they dried out? Who will remember to prune our almond trees? Who will listen to the singing of the nightingale?"

The wisest of the wise (Allah is wisest of all) counseled resignation.

"It's no use lamenting. You'll never again see the valley of the pomegranate and of the joy of life."

The leaders of the goums were sharply taken to task and accused of lacking vision.

"Why did you ally yourselves with the future losers?"

The most valiant of the standard-bearers stood up and explained to them that they could only rally behind the green banner of Islam.

"Long before the first confrontations, long before the first defeats, we knew that we were the weaker. But for the honor of the tribe and for the glory of Allah, we had to rise up. Would you have preferred that we deny our faith and side with the infidels?"

"Why didn't you win? Explain that to us. What was missing? Faith? We are fanatics. Men? We are legions. Weapons? We have them."

"No, none of those things."

"Well, then what?"

They were unable to respond.

Despite his critical state of health, brought on by his advanced age and the sufferings of the long march, our holy man left his tent and, raising his hand, imposed silence on everyone.

"We have become not only the weakest, but also the most vulnerable. Our existence is more fragile than the life of a newborn infant, who can be carried off by the slightest ailment. For the survival of the tribe, you have to arm yourselves with courage, perseverance, and humility, and entrust the destinies of the tribe not to the most valorous or the most bellicose, but to the wisest among you: they will know how to avoid the discord and clan rivalries, which express your nobility but will henceforth be fatal to you. You will have to trade the love of defiance and panache for the love of obscure effort. Yes, we have reached the end of our journey. This is where you have to settle. No one will dispute your right to this place of desolation, as you put it. You will settle here, shut yourselves off from the world, draw closer together, forget the things that keep you apart and focus on the things that make you one. You will practice intermarriage without flouting the law of the Messenger. It will be useless erecting high enceintes around you. From now on, they will offer woeful protection against the thundering cannon. Your best ramparts will be your Faith and solidarity. You will neither admit foreigners nor attack them, you will simply let them slide off the carapace of your indifference. You will abandon thought and its dangerous speculations and, instead, devote yourselves to the faith. Our Book is the only certitude. You will make it your single object of study and glossing and, in a forbidden place, you will lock up all those profane texts that dispute the Almighty's knowledge of the world. That is my final counsel, for I am soon to leave you."

He died several days later and was buried at the foot of the enormous olive tree that gave its name to the village.

The death of their spiritual guide plunged our forebears into great spiritual distress. They felt orphaned, helpless, at the mercy of the misfortunes of the world. Dreadful was their sense of loneliness. The women's sorrow bordered on hysteria. The most fatalistic people drifted into an indolent stupor that robbed them of their love of life. The most dissatisfied resumed their ranting and railing, certain that the hand and authority of the patriarch would no longer inflict silence and obedience upon them. Those who detested the idea of bowing to the tutelage of the infidels suggested that they continue their march and place themselves under the protection of the nearest Moslem sultan.

Those who disagreed reminded them of what our holy man had told us.

"We always wait for someone else to lend us a helping hand. Algiers, which was considered untakable, surrendered in three weeks, and the Turk himself beats a retreat wherever the invincible armies land, the forces of those who have become the masters of fire and sword."

"Do you know what awaits you here? Warriors in caps and uniforms and with curled-up mustaches will come and dictate the new laws and you will have to knuckle under. You will count the price of defeat in sacks of grain that will be heavier than the weight of misery, in heads of cattle that will be more numerous then the stars in the sky, in heaps of gold and silver that will be higher than these mountains. They will talk to you on horseback in the tongue of the Roumi. Let us move on. Immense are the lands of Islam, and their sultans are still powerful. We will find another happy valley where clove and jasmine blossom.

"Sooner or later, those same armies will emerge here or there. The world belongs to them. We must stop fleeing this present day, which smacks of disaster. We have to forget the valley of rose laurel and dewy mornings and try to start all over again."

The most indecisive asked, "But where are we heading? Are we going to continue toward the south and cross the desert of sand, then the desert of stone, then the desolate bush and the realm of the Zandjs, and finally end up in the kingdom of Timbuktu? Or are we going to strike off toward the west and cross mountain after mountain, swollen rivers and arid plains, jungles swarming with wild beasts, in hopes of reaching the admirable city of Fez and its almond orchards? How many days of tormented marching and cold nights of exposure to all dangers? Hunger and thirst, pillagers and savage animals, fatigue and epidemics? And what about our aged men, our pregnant women, our sick, our children?"

Those most intent on continuing were, of course, the freest or the most able-bodied—unmarried adolescents or adults in the prime of life, but also people of humble backgrounds, merchants or artisans not subject to military service, plus the most adventurous, who thrilled at the thought of discovering so many new countries, and, last but not least, the most bellicose, who dreamed of encountering another banner under which to wage further wars.

They separated in sorrow. A mother, her face bathed in tears, watched the tenderest fruit of her womb marching off; a broken-hearted brother resigned himself to the departure of his comrade; a betrothed maiden went to hide her weeping and suffering behind a bush. Promised to one man, she had to give herself to another, and even provide him with as many offspring as possible.

Although certain they would never meet again, they nevertheless managed to beguile themselves with hope.

"We will settle in a country of Islam, we will purchase land and cattle, and, when the time comes, we will send you our guides and messengers, who will lead you to us. And our reunited tribe will experience new vigor."

Those who decided to remain insisted on giving them all their gold and silver, even the jewels of the women, even those of betrothed maidens, and they loaded them down with all the food they could carry.

"May Allah accompany you," they told them. "If fate goes against you, if the natives reject you everywhere, you know that as a last resort you will find brothers here, who, without sarcasm, will welcome the survivors of the adventure. However long you remain, however far you travel, you will have first pick of our maidens."

At the moment of farewells, only Allah could tell what was going on in all hearts.

With the aid of nostalgia, our forebears felt that by working relentlessly, they could create a second happy valley teeming with primroses and warblers and all the things that would make it an earthly rival of paradise, aside from the rivers of honey and the maidens with black eyes. In retreating, our forebears had taken along all varieties of plants and grains and many others, all sorts of animals, horned and unhorned, two-legged and four-legged, and many others. But neither flora nor fauna survived for long, not to mention the travelers who failed to endure the journey.

The mint slips and pomegranate stalks drooped and wilted despite the loving care lavished upon them, and the medlars and thujas withered. The wheat never managed to become acclimated, the barley yielded ten times less than in the valley of myrtle and bounty, where some of our fathers had lived without tilling or sowing for years because their silos were bursting.

However, a miracle occurred. Nearly all the eucalyptus roots took hold, and soon the shrubs began rising elegantly toward the sky. Within a few years, they formed a magnificent forest, which became a refuge for the birds of the surrounding area.

Our forebears discovered the virtues of local plants, the olive tree with its hard, hard wood, the fig tree with its gnarled branches. The former supplied them with oil and soap, the dried fruit of the latter was the core of their provisions for winters of cold and famine.

The delicate cows and the indolent sheep, which refused

to browse on briar, gave way to goats, which are so skilled at finding food.

Our ancestors had to get rid of their horses, which were useless now.

It was tragic.

That was the moment when they truly grasped the harrowing necessities of readaption.

The leaders of the çofs (regiments), the sons of the grand tents, the sharifs, the standard-bearers, the leaders of the goums, the emeritus warriors were relegated to the rank of foot-sloggers, ground-level, exposing their feet in dust and mud, clumping and drudging like clodhoppers. How could a man live without a horse? How could he face the eyes of men who stare at you from their coursers? How could he pursue the boar or the gazelle?

Farewell, farewell to jousts and races, and all those parades of as many as ten times a hundred horses, all caparisoned in gold-embroidered silk, snorting and stamping, more impatient than their masters, while the maidens, on their camels, peered through the curtains of their palanquins, eying the distant cavaliers, who, in the setting sun, were clad in an aura of golden dust, a nimbus of infinite seductiveness. Farewell to those wedding ceremonies in which luxury vied with lavishness, and the bride was squired to her new home by a host of riders, all of them sharifs and all of them bachelors, who returned, exhausted, at the end of the nuptials, after seven days and seven nights of libations and cavalcades.

Above all, our forebears realized that they would never again gallop across the battlefield, and that they would have to trade the scimitar and the rifle for the plow and the pick, their steeds for long-suffering donkeys or agile mules, and, even more so, arrogance for economy, beauty for utility.

The most elegant forgot how to show off their assurance, the most handsome their charm, the most lyrical their talent.

They built stone houses and settled down into resignation.

The first few years in Zitouna were murderous. The exiles discovered the new ardor of the sun, and then the cruel winter, with snow, oh what snow, several feet deep, covering the ground, crumbling and melting in your hand, yet persisting for months and months, starving the wolf in the forest, the bird in the sky, the rabbit in its hole. And also man.

Necessity forges virtue. The warriors found they were farmers. They put their shoulders to the wheel. But the stingy earth discouraged all efforts. The scrawny olive trees hopelessly refused to grow, driving even the most patient men to their breaking point; the barley spikes remained hopelessly meager; the goats were never more than skin and bones. Even the most stout-hearted eventually lost heart.

"We'll never get anything out of this calamitous soil. We would have been better off following our brothers."

"Do you know what dangers they've encountered?" was the reply. "Do you know what they've suffered? Foreigners up against the distrust and hostility of the inhabitants, reduced to begging for hospitality or mere tolerance?"

"But they haven't come back. They must have discovered another valley teeming with carnations and ringdoves."

And in the face of so much harshness, the drill of hope for outside help began insidiously boring into their minds. They started counting the months that had worn by since the departure of their brethren, they started gauging the distances to a possible haven. Their eyes unwittingly scanned the horizon that had swallowed up their companions, and more and more often they caught themselves scrutinizing the road on which the others had disappeared.

The glimpse of the vaguest shadow quivering in the distance set the village all aflutter.

But year followed year, and nobody came. So much disappointment exhausted even the most willing arms. No one had the heart to clear the undergrowth, dig wells, plant trees, work the plow.

Shriveling into themselves, they huddled into an interim and lived from waiting.

THE ADOLESCENT had long been watching the black car as it laboriously toiled its way up the slope, endlessly zigzagging to avoid the gullies and potholes. He dashed over to the fig-tree square in order to warn us.

The entire male populace was already assembled when the chromium-plated snout of the limousine appeared at the end of its climb and slowly nosed into the only street in the village. We were fascinated by the silent gliding of the vehicle, which seemed to be moved by the magic of authority. The wheels stopped turning several yards from the village agora. After several minutes of petrifying suspense, the door opened, emitting a formidable expletive.

"Shit! This village is harder to reach than the gardens of paradise."

The broken body had a difficult time extirpating itself from the car before it was able to straighten up. And the immense stature of Omar El Mabrouk hove into view.

The oldest among us began trembling.

A fantastic reappearance. An incredible resurrection. He stood there scowling at us, his face dripping with sweat. Omar El Mabrouk, who we had thought was dead.

We all remembered Omar El Mabrouk's childhood, and even more his tumultuous ancestry. You can judge the harvest by the seed. Let me tell you the story of his grandfather, Hassan El Mabrouk the terrible, whose abuses sowed confusion in our area. The teenager feared neither God nor adults. Early on, he became an expert in the art of wielding the stick, and he terrorized all the solitary inhabitants of the region, robbing the farmers he met on the roads, assaulting the cattle dealers returning from the livestock market in Sidi Bounemeur. At the advice of the village sages, Hassan's father, hoping to get his unruly youngster to settle down, provided him with a wife before he even reached his fifteenth birthday. But within six months, the long-limbed adolescent's spouse died—supposedly of sheer delight. His second bedmate passed away even sooner. The most credulous of the villagers, and all our women, took stock by the rumor that began to circulate. Supposedly, the giant's member was so phenomenal that it pierced the innards of any female submitting to it.

However, from his earliest years, Hassan had had eyes only for the older sister of Aïssa the cripple. Long before puberty, she grew so tall that the village soon agreed unanimously, save for one vote, that she could be wed only to the vigorous widower.

The virgin's father did not share this opinion. He regarded Hassan as a rogue who feared neither God nor man, and he obstinately refused to yield his daughter. It was no use interceding, negotiating, compromising—Aïssa's father turned a deaf ear.

"I'm not handing my child over to that scoundrel."

Vexed, Hassan's father stood up, ending the discussion.

It was a dreadful winter night, with the snow piling up, the wind howling, and the cold so cutting that the shrew decided to burn her goat's horns as fuel in order to warm herself.

The door was kicked open, admitting the double-barreled gun illuminated by the candle that Aïssa's father had lit. Brandishing a skittish rifle, Hassan grabbed the girl's wrist and disappeared into the nightly turmoil.

The mother's lamentations awoke the villagers. Her husband armed himself with a club and went to bang on the door of Hassan's father, who would have been struck down but for the prompt intervention of several neighbors who held back the body if not the fury of the man whose honor had been sullied. They preached appeasement. The imam's intervention quieted the dispute. Aïssa's father agreed to describe what had happened. Since it had started raining, they decided to head for the hall of the mosque.

When called upon to explain, Hassan's sire displayed a brutal frankness.

"You know very well I can't control that hooligan. It's not for lack of trying. I condemn what he's done as much as you do. First of all, that man has sullied my honor. Tomorrow, if you like, we'll go and beat the woods until we find him. And I swear to you that when we flush him out, my finger won't hesitate to squeeze the trigger."

The battue proved useless, to the great relief of not only those not involved, but also Aïssa's father, who was terrified by the prospect of a killing, as well as Hassan's father, who was scared of having to keep his word.

Many of us, you see, were of two minds about the incident. While severely condemning the procedure, most of us agreed that they made a lovely couple. And we were not so simpleminded as to believe that the giant boy could have so easily carried off the giant girl.

As a matter of fact, she revealed an unexpected docility. She went along with Hassan, not really showing much resistance, and in the grotto sheltering them, he could never have approached her without her consent.

During the first few lovely days, Hassan built an adobe

shanty in the forest. The hovel of the two titans often rang
with the racket of their hue and cry. The man felt he was
in a conquered country. His spouse, outside of bed, had not
learned how to remain passive. Peppery was he, and pun-
gent she. Very often, the husband's unforeseeable slap only
encountered the wife's parrying arm. The Hercules was
quick to grab the stick hanging from a nail in the adobe
wall—until the day his gigantic darling, more nimble than
he, snatched the stick and, with her bare hands, broke it
more easily than a grape shoot.

Above and beyond Hassan, Aïssa's sister kept two cows,
which had grown so fat that they aroused a lot of envy. At
dawn after a stormy night, when Hassan opened his eyes at
the first call to prayers, he noticed the abnormal light that
was bathing the house. His wife, who instantly awoke, let
out a shriek. Jumping to their feet, they gaped at the huge
breach in the opposite wall. The cows had vanished.

Hassan was sure of it: his home had been raided by the
Beni Hadjar. They were the only ones who could operate
so discreetly. Without saying a word, he pulled on his burnoose, unhooked his new stick, and strode out.

The tribe of the Beni Hadjar had experienced a fate that
was similar to ours. After being conquered, they had taken
refuge on an even more desolate and inaccessible peak,
which faced us from the other side of the great precipice.
However, those men never benefited from the teachings of
their sages. Turning their back on the recommendations of
the Lawgiver, they preferred devoting themselves to pillage
and highway robbery. Allah punished them by marking
them with blazing hair, so that everyone could recognize
them. Big noses made them look like birds of prey. Easily
identified by their inevitable yellow turbans, they scoured
the countryside in gangs of four or five men, silent, furtive,
evanescent, popping up and disappearing, as if capable of

being everywhere at once. Their cruelty was legendary.
They never spared their victims. When they suddenly
turned up, blocking the way for a farmer who was carting
his harvest to market or, more frequently, returning with
the proceeds carefully bulwarked in his armpit, the man
knew he was doomed.

In the past, they had frequently raided the livestock
market in Sidi Bounemeur. Upon their arrival, voices faded
out, transactions sped up, haggling broke off, numerous
buyers slipped away, rescheduling their plans for some other
week. The Beni Hadjar showed up, one by one, and began
strolling among men and beasts: serene, indifferent, alien,
and silent. Then, moments later, they would straggle away
just as nonchalantly and melt into the natural surroundings.
They had no need to talk, signal one another, put their heads
together. They had tacitly agreed on their prey. The jittery
dealer or breeder could contrive to change his itinerary by
going home along the most unexpected, most circuitous
roads. At the fixed moment, they would loom up before him,
still calm, almost indolent, still taciturn.

Sometimes, for reasons known only to themselves, they
would attack on the spot and on the spur of the moment.
Pouring into the marketplace from many sides, they would
gradually surround their quarry, then strike lightning-fast.
Their victim was killed and robbed, and none of the onlookers dared to stir. The raiders then slowly drifted off. The
squads of gendarmes never acted very eager to pursue them;
they knew how dangerous it was to confront these men who
seemed to have nothing but contempt for life, who fought
methodically and casually, murdering placidly or dying
without a peep. These sons of the devil abandoned their
dead without a twinge of remorse, leaving the cadavers as
food for hyenas and crows. The administrator of the joint
parish reacted only when the Beni Hadjar attacked coloni-

als. Invoking the principle of collective responsibility, he would send the gendarmes out to the rugged peak, and they would bring back a dozen male adults with halters round their necks. The prisoners were sentenced to years of breaking rocks in quarries, digging galleries in mines, or picking halfa grass—unless the court decided to transport them across the ocean. Thus, the number of males in their tribe kept shrinking nonstop.

These were men without religion. They had no imam or mosque, they never prayed or fasted, and even the most learned among them was incapable or reciting so much as the shortest sura in the Koran. Rumor had it that they didn't know how to cut the throats of their animals, so they simply brained or strangled them before slicing them up. It was actually claimed that they never buried their dead. May they be cursed!

Since more and more of their women remained unmarried, the tribe sent them to the garrison towns, where they gave themselves to spahis and goums for drachmas and deniers. The most expert women taught the debutantes the secret gestures that inflame the body and ensnare the mind. Their skills brought them such renown that visitors arrived from the most distant places. These girls knew how to arouse the wildest desires, and they not only indulged any and all whims, they actively encouraged them. The nights of these towns were often disrupted by the brawls of men scuffling for their favors. Some of these men were so obsessed that they wanted to marry them. The guardians of these sorceresses demanded a high price for their consent. But, more often than not, when soldiers who'd received their pay or livestock breeders who'd made a profitable deal were drawn to them, then after the wine, the singing, the dancing, after the postcoital languor, their throats were slit and their purses filched by some man emerging surreptitiously. The remains of the corpse, destined for the vultures, were found several days later at the bottom of a ravine. The military authorities, puzzled by these strange demises of their rank and file, conducted a thorough investigation. But despite their suspicions, they never managed to prove anything.

Among themselves, the Beni Hadjar, ignoring the shalt-nots of the Apostle, shameless practiced adultery and incest, so that after multiple fornications, they no longer knew from which mother-of-pearl drops their children had issued.

Hassan El Mabrouk was convinced that only the men of the tribe of the Beni Hadjar could have so silently dug a hole in an adobe wall, untied the animals, and stolen away with them. No one was more intimate with our region than Hassan. Striking off along various paths, he crossed the only bridge over the precipice separating our countryside from that of those hell-bound men; then he stationed himself under a bush. He waited until the three men leading the cows reached the middle of the bridge. Now, with his left arm wrapped in his burnoose and his right arm brandishing the stick, the giant burst from his hiding-place. Immense and vehement, he shouted to an imaginary accomplice, "Block them on your side!"

And, at the other end of the bridge, a second giant loomed up, his left arm wrapped in his burnoose, his right arm brandishing a stick.

"I'm here!"

The olive sticks swung into action, and the three bludgeoned thieves tumbled over the parapet.

All along the way home, Hassan El Mabrouk kept fulminating against his wife, who had had the audacity to put on his clothes.

"How could you dare?"

"How could you have managed without my help?"

"You're nothing but an adventuress. I wonder how you spend your time when I'm away from home."

"Guarding your cows, that's how."

Hassan's third wife passed away in turn after presenting him with an infant who was so puny and sickly that the titan cried shame. One day, he charged into the fig-tree square and, clutching the dwarf in the palm of his hand, he railed and ranted at Aïssa's father. "I'm returning the fruit of your licentious daughter. This teeny-weensy grub is not the product of my flesh."

Profoundly upset, Hassan El Mabrouk was not long in following in the footsteps of the men who had tried to steal his cows. He went back to stalking our mountain roads, looting and robbing anyone who had the misfortune to come his way. The gendarmes paid us several visits, accusing us of sheltering and feeding him, whereas if our sages encountered him, they would always exhort him to go back to the straight and narrow path.

Then Hassan El Mabrouk vanished altogether. Neither he nor his crimes were ever heard of again. It was asserted that he had finally joined the Beni Hadjar, marrying one of their women and living their life-style. May God help those who have gone astray and lead them back to the path of righteousness!

That was the reason we felt so apprehensive as we watched the rickety offspring of Hassan El Mabrouk growing up in his maternal grandfather's home. After three difficult years, the child began to shoot up more briskly than, in the spring-time, the branches of pomegranate trees gorged with water from the valley of tulips and happy memories. However, we were relieved to note that, in contrast with his father, Slimane was calm, sedate, respectful, and obedient—indeed, so much so, that his grandmother often held him up as an example to her turbulent progeny. It is well known that ashes are born from fire. The boy would frequently spend hours and hours sitting by the threshold, immobile and silent, as if lost in profound meditation. He refused to take part in the violent games of his Uncle Aïssa, the clubfoot, who was one year his senior. Slimane was a child of few words, responding to questions tersely and soberly. He had no friend, no companion. His grandfather began to wonder how long this peculiar conduct would last.

"Was my older daughter really seduced by some highwayman passing near the couple's cabin?"

Finally, one evening, after he kept watching Slimane methodically helping himself from the common plate of couscous, his guardian said, "I believe the boy is a bit simpleminded."

The utterance of this oracle put a whole new complexion on things. People now lost interest in Slimane's eccentricity. The neighboring women stopped pitying the orphan, Aïssa stopped asking him to join his games; his aunt no longer touted him as an example, and little Meriem, who was already diabolically seductive, no longer made eyes at him.

Slimane thus lived in the home of Aïssa's father, as a neutral and transparent presence, a familiar and taciturn shadow, growing up amid general indifference. Whenever his grandfather went to the Sidi Bounemeur market to sell off his surplus olives or barley, he would first put aside the necessary money for settling his bill with the grocer and then deck out his household in new clothes. However, upon returning home, he realized that he had, in all good faith, completely overlooked Slimane. Being a man of great equity, he felt obliged to return to the village and bring the orphan a few items identical with what he had gotten for his sons. They had even almost forgotten to have him circumcised. It was only at the last minute that he was hastily wrapped in a borrowed gandoura and taken along with Aïssa, who blubbered away, indifferent to the words of the adults who tried to distract him and placed dirty and crumpled banknotes in his lap. The child let out a piercing shriek the instant his legs were pulled apart. But the burnoose embroiderer was already rising, with almost no blood on his razor. There was a moment of wavering when they nudged Slimane in the back and he moved forward. Who was going to hold down this brawny boy? But Slimane submitted with a detachment that drew admiring murmurs from the onlookers.

When Slimane turned five, the imam refused to admit him to the Koran school. He told Aïssa's father, "The union between Hassan and your daughter never received the fatiha. Thus this boy was born of adultery. He cannot cross the threshold of God's house to receive His Message."

Slimane's guardian did not protest excessively; instead, he ordered the boy to start tending the family goats.

Several months later, Aïssa's father was delighted to see that the animals were giving far more milk than before, and that a thick layer of fat was covering their once protruding bones. During that same year, six females gave birth. And, that, as I have determined, is something you can ask my son about.

"The innocent have always enjoyed divine favor," several begrudgers commented.

The happy beneficiary never dreamed of contradicting them. After long negotiations, he agreed to let the imam and two other breeders entrust their flocks to Slimane in exchange for a percentage of the kids. The boy thus found

himself with a good hundred animals, which he led at the
crack of dawn toward more and more distant flanks of
mountains that were still green.

However, the orphan grew terribly fast, and by twelve
he had reached a man's stature. On the day of Aïd, the
holiday commemorating Abraham's sacrifice, he borrowed
a burnoose from his uncle and attended morning prayers in
the mosque at the same time as we did. When he arrived, the
imam pushed him back with a gesture.

"You cannot enter these premises."

Slimane lowered his head and silently slunk away. He
took refuge in the shade of an olive tree and cried his eyes
out. Many of us regretted the intransigence of our sheik.

The boy's adoptive father was faced with a problem of
conscience.

"Slimane is now a man," he told his wife. "It makes no
difference that he's simpleminded, I can't very well keep
having him tend our goats. That's not a fit occupation for
an adult."

Our imam readily agreed. He suggested having Slimane
lead his plow oxen.

"Ahmed, my plowman, doesn't want to have his son do
it anymore. I'll offer the job to Slimane."

A younger uncle thus received the goatherd's crook
from his predecessor, and Slimane was initiated into the art
of commanding two yoked beasts. Several days later, the
plowman agreed to let him hold the stilt of the plow for brief
interludes. After the inevitable blunders of training, Slimane
succeeded in drawing straight furrows that were twice as
deep.

"You're damn strong, my boy," said his admiring companion.

Aïssa's father was not the last to realize his grandson's
dexterity, and, upon seeing him work the plow more and

more often, he went to the imam to request a pay raise for his protégé. He was given a categorical refusal.

After mulling for several days, the boy's guardian made an announcement to his wife; his tone was innocuous but resolute, to make it clear that he was not consulting her, but merely informing her of a decision that he had already reached: "I'm going to sell all my goats, borrow the rest from my brother, and go to Sidi Bounemeur to buy a pair of oxen. Slimane has turned out to be a first-rate plowman. He's capable of turning over about two and a half acres a day, and deep into the soil at that. We can make a lot of money hiring out our services, the way the imam does, for a tenth of the harvest."

"Your brother is famous for his greed," his wife replied. "He won't give you a duro."

"I'll give him part of my olive trees as collateral."

"The sheik won't appreciate the competition."

"I won't lose any sleep over that."

Slimane gained on the deal, for he inherited a real plow equipped with two stilts that could be pressed down solidly and an iron share that sliced through a suddenly softened earth.

When the plowing was done, Slimane asked his protector if he could reclaim the wedge of garigue that belonged to the family but had always been neglected.

"That would be a titanic labor, and the results would probably be disappointing. I'd be amazed if anything whatsoever could be grown on that patch of gravel."

"What else can I do all day long?"

"Whatever you like."

At the age of fifteen, Slimane adopted a lifestyle that he was to maintain until his dying day. He would rise at the crack of dawn, with the first cry of the muezzin. After performing his religious duties outside the mosque, he would bolt down a huge plate of couscous laced with goat's milk, cram three barley biscuits and two handfuls of dried figs into the hood of his burnoose, and then head toward the fields and not come back until the dead of night. He would turn in immediately after wolfing down his last mouthful of supper. Unlike all other teenage boys, he never felt a need to go to town in order to indulge in bad habits and luxuriate in furtively leering from afar at a colonist's daughter or forcing himself to swig a few gulps of that bitter, bubbly, and nauseating liquid. He allowed himself to rest only on religious holidays, less out of piety than to avoid incurring the imam's anathema.

At eighteen, Slimane was almost one foot taller than the lankiest youngsters in the village, and whenever he strode by, the admiring oldsters would comment:

"It's wonderful to see that he has put his vigor in the service of goodness."

"I think it's time he was provided with a wife. His ardor will work wonders in bed too, and we'll soon see some robust males swelling our ranks."

His grandfather, who realized how much his new prosperity owed to Slimane's formidable activity, held his tongue. After some resistance, he finally gave in to the advice of the djemaa, which was influenced by the imam, who had hit on this tactic for eliminating his competitor.

"A fine idea," the grandfather replied, "my daughter Meriem has just reached puberty."

They pointed out that it was unbecoming for a man to marry his own aunt, even if she was younger than he, even if she was still a virgin.

Aïssa's father was not convinced. But Meriem, coquettish as ever, now had a crush on Rabah, a handsome boy who would eventually become a country constable and the second village official next to the son of Ali. So the girl explained to her mother that she did not care to find herself in bed with a man who was twice her size; otherwise she might suffer the same fate as her older sister, who actually had a far greater advantage over her in corpulence. Aïssa's mother pleaded with her husband, finally persuading him to abandon the idea. He then began to consult the fathers of marriageable virgins. Eventually, he chose the one whose father showed the greatest understanding. However, when the proposal was officially stated and accepted, the future father-in-law, who realized what a force of nature he would be linked with, publicly demanded that Slimane enjoy his full inheritance rights.

"The family legacy," Aïssa's father protested, "has to remain a joint possession, according to the dispositions of our ancestors."

The issue, he was told, was not to break up the patriarchal property, but to have Slimane enjoy the share coming to him from his brigand of a father.

"Since you took charge of the boy, it was only fair of you to benefit from his goods and chattels. But now that he's about to set up his own household, they ought to be reassigned to him."

The grandfather argued that he had raised Slimane like his own son, so that, logically, his portion should be no greater than what each of his uncles could lay claim to.

The assembly thrashed it out for a long time. They cited the rules of the Lawgiver, they invoked the customary arrangements, they asked our best memorialists to recall the precedents. It was a rip-roaring controversy. As usual, agreement was reached on the basis of a compromise. When the young man was finally asked to voice his opinion, he expressed his total approval of their decision, his eternal gratitude to his guardian, and his profound thanks to the assembly.

The members of the djemaa congratulated themselves
and one another for this excellent conclusion to the affair
and, in order to celebrate the event, Aïssa's father and Slimane's father-in-law each slaughtered a goat.

With the help of his uncles and in-laws, Slimane built a
stone house, and the marriage ceremony took place with
proper simplicity. The morning after the wedding night,
Slimane went back to work.

His grandfather's anxieties proved groundless, for the
giant could be found more often in the adjacent fields than
in his own, helping out his sluggish uncles; just as he considered it a matter of course to continue plowing for the man
who had once taken him in, and who was visibly becoming
more and more prosperous, especially since his numerous
sons were now all pitching in.

Thus, after a conflict with the Jewish merchant of Sidi
Bounemeur, to whom he used to give his olive harvest, he
decided to purchase his own oil press.

"It'll be an excellent deal," he told his wife.

"In what way?"

"Nobody in Zitouna will dare refuse to bring me his
harvest. At the end of the season, I'll rent a wagon and
transport my oil to the cities of the plain. You probably don't
realize it, but the Roumis are still at war, and still fighting
the Germans, according to Georgeaud, and he knows what
he's talking about. They've started rationing goods. That
explains why our grocer no longer receives sugar or coffee.
In those seaside towns, the juice of my olives will be worth
its weight in gold."

Every year, Slimane handed his grandfather and his
father-in-law one third of his barley and olive harvests,
against his wife's better judgment.

"We've got more than we need," he remarked.

"You have to think about conserving your strength and

your income. Time flies, old age comes, and it'll make you as feeble as a newborn baby."

Slimane's spouse died after bearing him two children. He insisted on digging the grave himself for the woman who had just left him after a brief conjugal life filled with patience, attentiveness, and gentle submission. We were overwhelmed by the sight of the colossus as he picked up the so-slight corpse and placed it with infinite caution on the bottom of the hole.

Slimane grew even more tight-lipped and worked twice as fiercely. He refused to replace the dead woman, turning down all proposals that were made to him, and he entrusted his two children to his uncle Aïssa.

From then on, whenever anyone passed away, Slimane, without even being asked, put a pick and a shovel on his shoulder and headed toward the cemetery to prepare the grave.

"That man is a godsend," the village oldsters commented.

Now switch off your recorder, I have to rest a while and, above all, gather my reminiscences. Old age has ruined my memory. In any case, you haven't understood a thing I've said, otherwise you'd be impatient to find out what happened to Slimane, the father of Omar El Mabrouk, and curious to learn what that strange Gypsy was planning to do in our village.

YES, WHEN Omar El Mabrouk appeared in the village, so many of us recalled the predictions of that strange Gypsy— half-huckster, half-tumbler, with his wild prophet's beard and his long hair fluttering in the wind. He would visit our village every year, alternating between tricks and messianic or mocking harangues, ultimately extolling, without much conviction, the virtues of his liquid panacea in its small amber-hued vials. We thought he was Jewish because he spoke our language with an accent, but he managed, far more ably than the imam, to sprinkle sumptuous Koranic quotations throughout his speeches. His singular exegeses added a new significance to the divine tiding, and our sheik would very often smell a heretical commentary, but hold his peace, rather than having words with the redoubtable ora- tor, who had always succeeded in making fools of the pre- tentious barnstormers who dared to contradict him. He seemed to have reaped his immense and eclectic knowledge during his endless peregrinations.

"Listen, all of you, and mark my words. I am speaking for the future and I am never wrong. I have been alive for ten centuries, not counting the years, which are the dust of my age. Thus I have had more than enough time to visit the seven continents and commit the seven deadly sins. I know that you are pious farmers, preoccupied solely with the health of your goats, the condition of your olive trees, and the recitation of your five daily prayers. You would freeze with horror if I told you the price I had to pay for the dreadful secrets of the world that I wanted to ferret out. At the age of seven, I slipped a scorpion into the bed of my mother, who incessantly fornicated with passing strangers, and, fulfilling the prediction, I strangled my father when the circumference of the orange tree that I had planted was as large as his neck. I belonged to the sect of the Assassins, of sinister memory. Together we terrorized vast domains, hordes of us descending on villages to slaughter the babes-in-arms and the men of wisdom. During three journeys to the country of the Zandjs, I amassed a fortune that was heavier than your resignation. I used it to arm three solid ships and liberate the syphilitics exiled to their distant isle. The instant we landed, they were eager to spread their treponemata throughout the world. And those were the least of my atrocities. I am telling you all this so you may know the cost of the knowledge concentrated in these flagons, which I will presently be giving away for two sous apiece."

He paused in order to let us shiver.

"I have known the seven parts of the world. I have traveled the lands where people walk on their heads, those that have winter in summer and summer in winter, those that have night in the day and day in the night, those whose inhabitants can die only of madness, stricken with an uncontrollable laughter that is reflected from place to place by the silver surfaces of their mirrors. I have spent fifteen months on the isle of Waq Waq, where the trees bear fruits with human faces. I have discovered the woodlands with a suffocating atmosphere, where the wings of mosquito swarms murmur such a soft lullaby that the natives die because they are unable to wake up again. I have visited the everlasting islands, which can be reached only unexpectedly, and where the inhabitants feed only on barley, raising goats that they allow to die of old age and fighting one another by throwing stones. I have voyaged as far as the feverish places where the sun never sets, dooming men and women to wear themselves out with insomnia until they collapse from their fatigue upon a snow that never melts. I have climbed El Qummur, the highest mountain in the world, to greet the people of the land of Ashash, who fiercely guard the most precious secret on earth. They order repugnant caterpillars to spin silk and they alone know how to fabricate the fine and soft cloth you use for your turbans. I have seen nations who still worship animals, and others who revere no God, who are happy with their freedom, and whose flabby and abulic males live suspended from the enormous bosoms of their spouses. Thus, like you, they make no politics, they are content to suck a milk of youth, which nullifies the effect of time and erases memory. Young and amnesic, they let their wives perform the tasks of attending to their daily keep and their existential reflections. Thanks to my opulent beard, I was able to leave unscathed the most hostile region, the lair of the hidden imam whose followers are more numerous than the stars in the sky, than the pebbles on the ground, and who, in their clandestine existence, affirm their faith by voluntarily scarifying their bodies and furbishing their weapons, thereby girding themselves to avenge the assassination of Hussein. Some day, they will sweep over you and, ruthless and shameless, they will make you suffer the fate of the child martyr. I have crossed the barrier erected by Alexander to contain the sons of Gog and Magog, those barbarians with immense ears capable of covering their entire bodies, those barbarians who will some day devastate the earth and drink up all the water of the lakes and rivers. Your lands will then revert to their primordial dryness. I know that you have had to forget History, the tragedy of subjugation, the pangs of misery, the doubts of the night. And yet, your unhappiness is only just beginning."

He fell silent for a moment, then stepped forward with a smile.

"I am here to entertain you, and you are not obliged to take my words seriously."

He showed up in Zitouna at the end of every summer, when earth and hope were crumbling into dust as if to make it even more painful for us to breathe. Our children sounded the alarm the instant his equipage appeared on the peak of the slope. Time and its disappointments had gradually rubbed out the gaudy inscriptions on the wagon drawn by an old nag that had likewise lost her glow of youth.

"Always accompanied by my faithful bear, I have knocked about all the seas in the world. I have sailed across oceans so deep that they could swallow up whole fleets with all hands, and no one would ever find a trace; oceans so vast that, by comparison, the one limiting your horizon looks like a puddle of water after a cloudburst; oceans so long to cross that the sailor falls in love with his wife again; oceans so fraught with danger that the miscreant discovers faith. I have navigated oceans that ebb and flow at the mercy of the moon, the way the loving fiancée dances upon learning that her exiled beloved will be coming home tomorrow. I have cruised the Dead Sea, which bears that name because no wave ever ruffles its surface, a surface smoother than a baby's cheek. Sterile serenity: its breasts nourish no fish. I have felt my ship buffeted on the billows which are tormented all year long by raging winds more disastrous than your suspicions of your wife's infidelity. I have fallen into the traps of oceans that imprison reckless adventurers. The tongs of their ice grip, that smash the hull of a boat more easily than my fingers can crush the shell of this egg you see here, more easily than my bear's paw can snap the neck of the strongest man among you. I have put my wagon on an immense dogsled and slid across the back of the world to find myself in the land where everything is the other way round. I have seen oceans so jammed with fish that they turn to gold in the setting sun, and I have seen others forever cloaked by mists that are denser than your ignorance and that drift about or end in places without issue, finding no land, like the promises of your future leaders. They will tell you that your forebears were the first to cross the ocean and discover America. Do not believe a word of it, even though it is quite possible. They know nothing about it, and you should be wary."

He parked his wagon on the fig-tree square and promptly ordered one of the boys standing around him to fetch him a large goglet of cool water.

"My bear and I have to cleanse our throats of this dust of desolation."

One summer, he arrived with a small bird of prey on his wrist.

"This is a kestrel, the most ferocious bird in the world. It never spares its victim. But it's also the most courageous. It attacks winged creatures four times its size. I am speaking to those who can catch the drift of my allusions."

He said all those things in the troubled times of war, yet no military hazard could have made him miss his annual rendezvous with the villagers. The puzzled soldiers, who watched him arduously climbing toward us, wondered what could possibly draw him to this place of exile and oblivion. He was frisked, his wagon was meticulously searched, he endured long interrogations. His tormentors were utterly perplexed by the mountebank's provocative responses.

"I am an agent of Moscow disguised as a Gypsy. I've come to see how the local revolutionaries are getting along. They've been trained at enormous expense in the best Soviet schools. After all, they're confronting an imperialist nation of middling power. Not so long ago, you experienced the efficiency of our best pupils over in Asia, among the rice paddies. Ask my bear, he'll confirm it all."

As for the underground fighters, they took him for a spy and attempted to kill him twice.

"You'll never get me. I'm protected by my bear and a diabolical immunity. Keep away from me, or I'll sick my kestrel on you, and it will rip your eyes out."

He seemed terribly amused by this perilous ambiguity. His words defied us.

"Yes, good people, who have come here to be entertained: at a sign from me, my kestrel will soar up before pouncing on its prey. Remember that victory often belongs to the more resolute and not the more powerful. I know that my words cannot penetrate your darkened minds. But I believe in the virtue of example. Soon, a frail fellow will come, and he will explain what I have said. He will be at the origin of everything that happens to you."

Another time, he brought a terrifying monster in his wagon.

"Come closer, come closer, and admire this masterpiece of nature."

Led by a chain that was attached to his collar, the gnome shuffled forward, wagging his enormous head. Our imam instantly began reeling off a series of Koranic verses in order to exorcise the apparition. We punctuated his litany with a resounding *Amin*.

"Oh, no, my fine believers, this is not the demon, this is not Iblis coming to earth in order to torment you. With everything you have suffered here below, you certainly won't have to make his acquaintance on the day of the Resurrection. Allah is merciful and, without a doubt, he will recognize extenuating circumstances for your peccadilloes. What you see before you is a human being. Do not be afraid of his empty sockets, my kestrel has gouged out his eyes, and do not be afraid of his simian mouth, which carnival people widened with a knife to provoke the laughter of children. You know very well that this monstrosity feeds the joy of little scoundrels."

He took the creature around once more, making us shiver to our hearts' content.

"The people who sold him to me claim that he issued from the belly of a queen who was forced to witness the outcome of some wild desire that she had slaked without envisioning the consequences. But I suspect they made up this legend in order to jack up his price."

He lapsed into silence, his mocking eyes darting from face to face.

"I'm going to let him strut his stuff."

The man fastened the leash to a ring on the wagon shaft and charged toward the back of the wagon.

"And remember," he yelled, turning his head, "don't try to approach him."

He returned several moments later with a rooster struggling furiously on his arm. The bird's cackling made the monster raise his head. The mountebank handed him the prey. The manikin gestured briskly, pawing the air. But at his third try, the gnarled fingers managed to grab the animal's neck, seize its wings, and feverishly rip it to shreds. The gnome greedily sank his incisors in the throbbing flesh, smearing blood all over his enormous mouth. Allowing the carnivore to finish his meal, the beaming man came forward in the half moon created for him by the spectators.

"Don't let your brats get within range of his paws. Otherwise they may suffer the same fate as the rooster."

Going off again, he returned with a violin.

"And now, a change of scene!"

He handed the instrument to the monster, who had just

finished wiping his chops. And we were amazed to hear some sweet and lovely music that seemed to perfectly express our nostalgia for the happy valley.

"I'll let each one of you draw his own moral."

Thus, the tumbler varied his tricks and harangues every year. But the bear never left him.

"And now, let me propose something to you, you good farmers of the most isolated village in the world. You are unaware of the honor that I pay you by making a point of visiting you year after year—I, whose renown attracts the crowds in the most prestigious cities on earth: Paris, the city of light and love; Moscow, more beautiful under snow than the bride who has perished on her wedding day and now lies in her winding sheet; Vienna, hieratic and suffocating under the sumptuousness of its past; London, more surprising than its sunny mornings; Istanbul with its myriad seductions on the shores of the Bosporus; Granada, whose loss you will never stop mourning; opulent Samarkand, stabbing the sky with the arrows of its cupolas; and Baghdad, the sorceress, at the center of the world; and Damascus, the coquette; and Jerusalem, city oh my city of all cities, more tender in the waning sunlight than the first embrace of the loving woman finding her beloved again, from the Mosque of Omar to the Wailing Wall, my most obscure desires gratified by a hand that stiffens at the scent of jasmine, city oh my city of my childhood, city oh my city of the childhood of the world, with your gardens more cheerful than a hope of paradise; and a thousand other cities all of which we have known, my faithful bear and I. Whenever I arrived, I was thronged and heard by the greatest philosophers, who, thanks to my daring theses, discovered roads inaccessible to their speculations, and the most famous theologians, whose soundest theories I refuted, and illustrious savants, whose eyebrows were whitened by study, and who were stunned by my knowledge, and the most skillful politicians, who wanted me to instruct them in the art of steering the commonwealth, who drank in my words like a rare elixir; but also, and above all, plebeians, the dumbfounded humble people, curious children delighting in their future astonishment, drudging housewives abandoning their homes and sporting their most beautiful, deliciously antiquated frocks, idle and demanding old men, and bantering adolescents who had come to furtively leer at the girls in airy clothing, itching to shiver with horror, and decent heads of families, seeking distraction from work more humdrum than life without love, and all sorts of hooligans drawn by the mob, cutpurses, pickpockets, shoplifters, wagon burglars, but also swaggerers, barnstormers, swashbucklers, blusterers, braggarts, braggadocios, fanfarons, blatherskites, bluffers, bigmouths, and finally musclemen, who strutted around on the proscenium, more swell-headed about their strength than carnival wrestlers, more boastful of their biceps than circus athletes—and yet my bear always fought them and won, my bear, who has never submitted to anyone, my bear, who is standing here right now, my bear, who repeats his challenge today, to all of you."

The orator fell silent, his gestures froze, letting the full impact of the fermata sink in, before he resumed.

"I know that you are nothing but humble peasants, solely preoccupied with obtaining your daily subsistence, which you have to wrest from a meager soil, just as I know so many other things about you, the harrowing misfortunes of your ancestors when they made up their minds to leave the valley of tulips and abundance and take refuge on these protective but sterile peaks, digging themselves in, compelled to trade hope for resignation, horse for donkey, sheep for goat, script for speech, knowledge for superstition, science for magic. I also know that the harshness of life wiped

out your love of games and jousts, that you admire strength
and skill only if they are useful. So I will not challenge you,
I will merely invite you to a friendly trial of strength. Any
man among you who succeeds in throwing my bear can be
assured of his glory. I will take a photo of him and I will
travel the world, singing his praises.

"Naturally, none of you has the nerve to approach the
bear. Come, come, a bit of courage! I promise to give the first
candidate twenty vials of my miraculous elixir."

The offer tempted no one.

After scrutinizing the onlookers for a long time, the
mountebank pointed at Slimane, who was watching the
scene from the last row.

"Hey you, the giant, would you like to measure your
strength against my bear's?"

Slimane, removing his burnoose, strode up for the encounter with the upright creature, which, having learned
its role, would always start growling and clawing the air the
instant its master proposed a bout.

The throng fell silent.

"Now here's a courageous man, who brings honor to the
village," the huckster yelled. "Since the match strikes me as
unequal, if you win I'll reward you with the revelation of
the mystery of Christ and the favor of a death before senility,
at twilight of a day in mellow spring. Step back, folks, step
back, give them the space they need. Man, I warn you, my
bear has never been beaten."

Yes, I myself, who am speaking to you, I can guarantee it,
I saw it with my own eyes: Slimane won. After returning
the bear to his wagon and gathering his belongings, the
bearded man said, "Today I have had the most mortifying
experience of my very long life. I have seen my bear thrown

for the first time. Every year at the same season, I will come back here to renew my challenge. I will not rest until your champion is on his knees."

And thus, at the end of every summer, the struggle between man and beast recommenced. Always the victor, Slimane eventually put this periodic clash in the same category as the great farm labors. Time wore by, but the ardor of the antagonists never waned.

Until the day that the man was brought to his knees.

"I could not admit defeat. I am going away now that my bear has prevailed against your jouster. You will never see me again."

Silently, Slimane picked up his burnoose and returned to his field. He was discovered the next day, leaning against the trunk of an olive tree. He had stopped breathing.

Yes, that was how he died, Slimane, the father of Omar El Mabrouk and blond Ourida—Slimane, who had grown up among the children of Aïssa the cripple.

Before disappearing, the mountebank added, "You ought to know that your troubles have now begun. The son saw his father rolling in the dust, and none of you dared to come to his aid. He will never forget."

"IT'S HOTTER than a goat's vagina," he declared, stepping out of the car.

And when, after removing his glasses to wipe his face, Omar El Mabrouk confronted us, we instantly recognized the hateful eyes of the child, staring at us through the gap between the three intertwined fig trees while his father lay on the ground, moaning under the weight of the bear. However, the boy's silhouette had changed. Our memories had retained the image of a gaunt, bony teenager with an obstinate brow, and we were staring at a rounded, graying man with full cheeks, a potbelly, chubby hands, and a throat whose cascade of creases unequivocally signaled a man who always ate his fill.

"It's so damn hot!" he repeated.

Putting his glasses back on, he walked toward us.

No, he did not go to the trouble of unmasking his eyes, as if he had forgotten that failure to do so was the grossest of incivilities, worse than passing someone without greeting him, worse than eating with the left hand.

Followed by all the oldsters, the imam walked toward him. Within two feet of the newcomer, the imam froze and imperceptibly bowed his head to offer his turban for the awaited kiss.

But Omar El Mabrouk straightened up, holding his face aloft as if to flee a nauseating odor.

After an embarrassed silence, our sheik declared:

"Welcome to our village."

Omar El Mabrouk turned his back on him and walked to the center of the square. His eyes, still protected, wandered all over before he said:

"I see that nothing has changed since my adolescence. Your village is still a pile of crap. It looks like a Mexican hamlet. All those shanties huddling around the square. You haven't even been able to set up a small monument for the dead, with a flag, to at least show that you're no longer living under the colonial yoke."

Then, choking back his incipient mirth:

"But, you will reply, what good would that monument do? You have no name to inscribe on it. It's true you are such big cowards that despite all the affronts you've suffered, not a single one of you ever thought of joining the underground and the freedom fighters, just as not a single one of you tried to help my father, who had just eaten the dust under the claws of the bear. Yet there were so many of you, and most of you were in the full vigor of manhood. And you never stopped praising the helpfulness of Slimane, who dug the graves for your dead, lent you a hand to dislodge the huge rocks from your fields, cut and hauled the tree trunks necessary for building houses for newlyweds. When my father agreed to face the beast, he was doing it to defend your honor. He died of it. It was your cowardice, and not the bear, that killed him.

His smile abruptly turned sardonic as he suggested:

"Since you thought I was dead, you could have erected a stele with my name engraved on it. That might have helped you get rid of me."

He began shaking his head solemnly.

"Perhaps you were right to put on airs. The upheaval eventually passed without harming you. But this strategy won't protect you from the yawning chasm of the future."

After hesitating for a moment, our municipal representative went to join him.

"I'm Mohamed. Do you remember me?"

For the second time, the prefect took off his opaque glasses, and Mohamed rediscovered those sharp, adamantine eyes shining with cruel derision.

"Of course, you're the son of Djelloul the blacksmith."

"No, Messaoud the Recruit."

"In any case, I remember that you were the biggest coward in the village. Always prudent enough to be the last to follow our escapades and always ready to dash off at the least sign of danger. Have you changed?"

"I am now deputy mayor in charge of the administration of Zitouna."

"Just as I said: always retreating. Where is your boss?"

"In Sidi Bounemeur, the county seat."

"You'll never change: always under someone else's tutelage, always second, always minors. You'll remain a seedy lot forever. I know what I'm talking about, I was born among you."

"I would like to welcome you."

"Thanks, but I've already been welcomed."

"I meant officially."

"And your worthy superior did not feel it was necessary to raise his ass from his armchair and welcome me here?"

"He *was* notified."

"Remind me to kick him out."

"Certainly."

"Which I know is bound to warm the cockles of your heart. You people live purely on constant rivalries. You rejected the Prophet because he came from among you. Your capacity for envy is infinite. Yes, I'll appoint you to replace him. An offer you cannot refuse. I can sense that you're already infected with the virus of power. But believe me, you won't rejoice for long. You will become its hostage and you will know absolute servility when I teach you how to worship the things you have repudiated and to repudiate the things you have worshiped."

Omar El Mabrouk furiously pulled off his tie, put his glasses back on, and began to stride along the street, peering at the approximate architecture of our shanties with their off-kilter walls, their lopsided doors, their contorted roofs.

Mohamed followed him at a distance.

"Even the sun beats down as hard as ever."

The son of Messaoud granted him a smile of complaisance.

"I believe that things will change rapidly now that you're here."

"You can count on it."

"We are very happy about it."

"I can see that you have remained the same perfect hypocrite that I used to know."

The son of the recruit lowered his head. He suddenly felt like turning his back and leaving this insulter in the lurch.

At that instant, a boy of about ten unexpectedly cannoned out of an alley that meandered amid the houses. The boy had constructed a reed propeller which he now tried to get whirling by running at full speed, his arm against the wind. The blades smashed into the prefect's paunch, and the pilot in training crashed, chin-first, in a brutal belly-landing.

"Goddam son of a bitch!" yelled the sprawling man.

And as the youngster tried to get up, the prefect kicked him so ruthlessly that the boy nearly took off for good.

"You dirty little shit! If I catch you, I'll fuck the shit out of you!"

Struggling to his feet, the boy, with a bleeding mouth

and a swollen cheek, dashed off full speed ahead.

"These snotnoses haven't changed either."

"That was my son," said Mohamed.

The prefect started walking again, with our official reluctantly tagging along behind him.

"I got screwed like a novice," said the prefect. "I don't give a damn about their prefecture. What I was hankering for was an ambassadorship. A huge salary, all in hard currency, a vast residence located in the heart of a capital and crawling with servants, a deluxe car with a chauffeur who has to cool his heels from dawn to dusk and then from dusk to dawn until I'm good and ready, a government expense account for wining and dining anyone I like, including my mistresses and young hippie girls passing through. I pick my mistresses up at official receptions and my hippies on the street when I go strolling after a drinking bout: my wife is constantly enthralled by her lavish boutiques, so she doesn't bug me while I scour the streets and the females. What a dream . . . ! But all they offered me was some country in the asshole of the world—a country so bland and unobtrusive that you won't find it on any map, and so democratic that it doesn't have a head of state. So who would I have given my credentials to? I would have died of boredom and homesickness. Naturally, I refused. They forgot all about me for a long time, and then finally they gave me this post without consulting me. It's a way of sending me back to my native douar. They played a really dirty trick on me, those bastards. As if I hadn't floundered in enough mud during my childhood. I'm going to be among dirt farmers who'll expect everything of me—they'll want me to reduce the heat of the sun or the harshness of the cold, they'll want me to make barren women bear children or get rain to fall or revive the dead limbs of cripples!"

The two men reached the outskirts of the village, where

the three mansions of former colonists were located.

"Who's occupying them now?" asked Omar El Mabrouk.

"That one's being used as a municipal annex and post office. The imam and I are sharing the second one."

"I see you don't deny yourselves anything. Like everywhere else, the village notables are the first to help themselves."

"The lawyer lives in the third villa."

"Lawyer? What lawyer?"

"The old lawyer."

"The little fellow? He's been ordered back here too? Serves him right. He'd still be minister if he hadn't been such a smartass. He's one of those men who think they can afford the luxury of a conscience. So he didn't realize that power and conscience are mutually exclusive? In any case, you're going to liberate the first two villas for me within forty-eight hours. My administration needs them to start setting up its departments."

"But—"

"But what?!" shouted Omar El Mabrouk with a frown.

"Where should we put up our families?"

"That's your business. These lodgings are government property, and you are occupying them illegally. You wouldn't want to remain in an irregular situation now that you're mayor of Zitouna."

"But—"

"What, goddammit? Haven't you retained anything of what I've just said? The time of attentive listening and blind obedience has come for you. No more discussions, no more objections. I command and you obey. Is that clear? Fine, I consider the matter closed."

Then, abruptly changing the subject, "Do you know what the only thing is that's changed in the village? The eucalyptuses have kept growing. Judging by their noise, their branches must be welcoming a million birds. It's really deafening. Doesn't that mess up your siesta?"

He checked his watch.

"It's getting late! This village is so far out of the way that coming here is a real trek. And to think I have to settle down here."

Omar El Mabrouk doubled back, walking faster, with the mayor-elect in tow. Upon arriving at the fig-tree square, he told us in a loud voice:

"Listen up, you all know me: I'm a son of this village. You can no longer say that you're forgotten, that you're rejects of the Revolution. From now on, the future is in your hands. Together we will build this country, prosperity and justice will reign, and the bougainvilleas and the laughter of children will flourish again all around you, as they did in the happy valley. An exalting task is awaiting us."

And he headed toward his car. He was in such a hurry that he stepped into a donkey turd, if you'll pardon the expression. Letting out a string of curses, he shook his shoe, then disappeared into his vehicle, which promptly lurched off.

"He didn't even ask us for news about his sister," the imam remarked.

We all remembered the hotheaded adolescence of Omar El Mabrouk. In their phony lethargy, like a crocodile lurking for its quarry, the old men on the fig-tree square had soon noticed the unruly character of the mischievous brat. They were scared he might inherit the propensities of his grandfather, the terrible Hassan El Mabrouk, whose story I have already told you.

We are modest, but not gullible. There are many things

that we never bring up, but that are constantly on our minds. Although we are anything but ignorant of the bestial or unnatural acts in which our offspring indulge, we believe that for morality's sake, we should never tolerate them in word or attitude, lest we make them commonplace. We are quick to detect the first signs of agitation in our teenage boys, and we then never fail to quickly marry them to young maidens. Our customs allow widows and divorcees to discreetly receive these rutting lads, provided they are clever enough to make sure that no fruits come of their labors. Thus, if such a woman is asked, she can get a new husband with no dishonor accruing to her or to him. However, each father urges his spouse to allusively warn his virginal boy of the dangers inherent in the charms of these lone women. Nevertheless, some boys do grow attached to them and even ask to marry them. This step elicits universal disapproval. Such marriages are not reasonable. They are seldom well-balanced.

We also know that during their travels to the cities of the plain, beyond the great river and beyond the railroad, our boys never fail to try those prohibited drinks that make them vomit or to visit those houses of joy where one loses not only one's money but also one's self-esteem. We never interfere, for we are convinced that they will return with some sense knocked into them; they will believe that during this brief lark they have drained all the pleasures of the world to the dregs.

But that scoundrel Omar was so assiduous and frenzied in those regrettable practices that the most diplomatic among us agreed to drop a hint to Omar's guardian, Aïssa the oil-presser. However, the old man could only raise his hands toward the sky.

"I pray to Allah to guide him back to the road of righteousness."

The rascal had no respect for adults, and sometimes he even went so far as to talk back when they reprimanded him. He did not hesitate to ogle passing women. At the age of five, he had refused to pasture his guardian's goats, just as he had had enough with the imam's first two lessons, after which he deserted the mats of the Koran school. There were no limits to the violence of his games. One day, hooking his two forefingers, he tore the lips of the older son of Djelloul the blacksmith. The poor child became so repulsive that later on it was very difficult finding him a maiden who was not handicapped in some way. His father's fortune proved extremely helpful in this respect. Omar stole, lied, and assaulted so much that our sages ordered his great-uncle to punish him severely. His wrists and ankles were bound, and he was left without food or water for several days. Omar pretended to be sorry, he swore he'd turn over a new leaf, he begged for forgiveness; but once he was free to move again, he went back to his old ways and acted more frenzied than ever before.

He continued roaming the stripped flanks of our mountains, robbing the wolf traps, pouncing on stray goats, and intimidating the young girls who went to fetch water at the spring.

He got into the habit of frequently going to Sidi Bounemeur to buy bottles of wine, which he guzzled under a bush; next he would station himself near the bridge and challenge all wayfarers to a fight.

"I'm gonna fuck the mother of anyone who comes and anyone who goes," he shouted, brandishing his stick.

His stature discouraged even a hint of resistance.

Once, by threatening her with a cudgel, Omar took Suzanne, the daughter of Martial, a colonist, into a hollow, where he raped her. When she returned home, she did not go to the police. But in a region like ours, everything eventually comes out.

Martial had come here shortly after the war that led
Georgeaud beyond the seas. The colonist bought the Calabrais property dirt-cheap. Calabrais, a latecomer, had
managed to obtain only a portion of the scurvy flanks of our
mountains. He tried to grow wheat, then tobacco, before
losing heart, mainly because none of us was willing to work
for him. Actually, he spent most of his income on green
liquor.

"I wouldn't hesitate to sell off all these arid flanks for the
price of an acre in the plain."

Martial accepted the deal. He was already laughing up
his sleeve the day the cart dumped all his belongings a few
feet away from the eucalyptus forest.

"Don't worry," he told us in his strange jargon. "I'm not
here to compete with you. I come from an area that's even
harsher than yours, and I have no desire to start growing
barley or raising goats. I know what drudgery that is."

And he began to snicker.

"I'm devoting myself to something far more profitable."

A funny guy, that Martial. What interested him was not
so much the Calabrais property per se as its proximity to the
huge forest covering the peaks of the neighboring mountains. He packed his mule down with a huge number of rifles
and wolf traps, then struck off toward the woods, where he
spent several weeks. When he returned, his mule was loaded
with furs, and Martial greeted every passing farmer with a
malicious laugh. After curing the hides, he let them dry in
the sun, apparently delighting in the miasmas that stank up
the village. Then he piled them in the cart and went off to
peddle them in Sidi Bounemeur.

"You'll see," he crowed, "you'll see."

Indeed, this strange commerce proved fruitful, and Martial soon prospered. His success increased the loudness of his

snickers, blurred the homeliness of his features very slightly, and inflated his thorax with its protruding ribs.

He set about enlarging the shanty he'd gotten from Calabrais; then, when the work was done, he asked a widow in Sidi Bounemeur to share his new fortune: he admired her valor in working, if not the homeliness of her body. Her first husband, a brakeman by trade, had been sliced in two by a wheel while shunting a railroad car. The torpor following a meal with too much wine prevented him from switching fast enough. When the railroad car backed up, it knocked him down. He smashed into a girder and went sprawling across the rails.

Swept off her feet by the godsend of Martial's proposal, the ugly widow didn't have to be asked twice. The bride settled in Zitouna and promptly undertook to reinspire her husband, who was beginning to go soft with success.

They had a daughter who managed to combine the hideous features of both parents.

One day, the fur trapper learned from his Sidi Bounemeur customer that he had a young competitor. Martial chose to burst into guffaws.

"A competitor? Do you really imagine that an ermine, a marten, a fox or a weasel, a hare or a wolf is easy to bag? I wish him lots of cunning."

On the way back, all his mirth vanished; the man with the glowering eyes was puzzled. Having become distrustful, he began counting the hides he left out to dry. Until the day the double barrel of a rifle lifted up Omar's chin.

Suzanne, who was standing in the doorway of the shed, let out a piercing shriek.

That was how Martial learned that his daughter and the adolescent were having an illicit affair. The father was unfazed by the revelation, but he was far less accepting of the disappearance of some of his furs. He tied the thief to a beam in the stockroom and began interrogating him. Then he went inside his house.

He came back to Omar the next day; his good humor was restored.

"Listen," he told him. "I've been thinking. I've decided not to hand you over to the police. If you enjoy rolling in the thistles with that troll Suzanne, then more power to you. I wouldn't want to deprive her of such a windfall. But I've got a proposition for you. I'm getting on, and those long rounds in the forest and those damp nights are harder and harder on my joints. Would you like to be my partner?"

Omar's first instinct was to regain his freedom. He instantly said yes.

"I'll teach you the art of laying traps, placing snares, shooting rabbits. With my experience and your youth, we'll strike it rich very quickly, I can guarantee it. You have no idea how crazy they are about these furs across the sea."

I have to describe Suzanne for you. As you know, the Roumis are all beautiful. In fact, they'd be perfect if it weren't for the indecent color of their eyes. But Allah apparently wanted to unite all human homeliness in that girl. Her body was thick and gross, and heavier than a millstone. She had her mother's clumsy bearing and the trapper's scowling, rheumy eyes. Her eyelids, which had no lashes, were permanently infected and they were the constant prey of flies. Her lackluster cheeks resembled dead autumn leaves. Her sparse, stringy hair made her greasy scalp shine in the sun. Her short lips revealed a harelip. She had the foul breath of all pork eaters, and a blue, that is, black skin. I'm being precise because we consider it unseemly to pronounce that word.

And yet Omar El Mabrouk moved in with them and spent his nights with that ghoul.

To look at Ourida, the scoundrel's younger sister, you couldn't help but believe that Redwan had been negligent and forgotten to close the gates of the garden of paradise, thus allowing an angel to escape.

In our regions, a complexion the color of ripe dates unequivocally signals a sun-baked farmer who spends his days slaving in the fields. For us, a pale epidermis is a sign of urbanity, aristocracy, fortune. The maidens with the lightest pigment are always the most desired, providing they offer a minimum of width in the hips and heaviness in the rump. With puberty, our girls start fleeing the rays of the sun and smearing their hands and faces with those unguents that revive a bright skin. People wondered whom Ourida took after: she was blonder than a head of grain on the day of its harvest, and her face shone like the moon at its full. Her soft gestures and honeyed words made her even more attractive. The girl seemed endowed with an uncommonly obliging and exquisitely polite nature. She never balked at fetching fresh water in the gugglet hanging from a branch of a fig tree. Always prompt with greetings and wishes, the child lit up the day for any adult who encountered her in the morning.

But while all these gifts delighted our eyes and ears, we were nevertheless worried as we watched Omar El Mabrouk's sister growing up. The fusion of so many charms was bound to stoke the flames of desire in our adolescent boys. We have learned to fear the disorder and tragedy of passions aroused by beauty. From our hot-blooded ancestors, we have inherited a love of challenges and prompt

actions. We kill for a word, a smile, a look. Deprived of
enemies, we had become trigger-happy toward one another.
A simple affront could spark interminable butchery.

However, Ourida seemed intent on ridiculing our anxieties. Her behavior was praiseworthy in every way. When
she reached the age at which our maidens feel the first
sensations of their bodies and begin to chastely excite their
cousins, Ourida refused to indulge in those games and became more discreet than ever. We realized that she was not
playing hard to get when she fled admiring looks and compliments.

Furthermore, she was the only person to whom her
good-for-nothing brother was willing to listen. He was indifferent to threats, blows, punishments, but a frown from
his sister was enough to dampen his ardor. The mere sound
of Ourida's voice could make the bellicose hooligan freeze,
with dangling arms, in the thick of a brawl. We often saw
the younger sister lead her suddenly mollified brother by the
hand. All the women made it a practice to complain to
Ourida about the rapscallion's harassment, and Aïssa himself
surreptitiously allowed her to educate the boy. But, as time
wore by, the reprobate escaped her influence more and
more. He came home less and less, preferring to spend his
days and nights gallivanting about the countryside, where
the girl could not very well pursue him.

When Ourida learned that Omar had moved into the
Martial home and was hunting wild animals for him and
sleeping with his daughter, she flew into such a fury that our
hearts quaked.

"Has he lost so much dignity that he can agree to work
for that miscreant? Is he so obsessed with the thing that he
can actually share a bed with a repugnant ghoul who never
shaves her groin and never washes herself after the act?"

She fulminated nonstop for half a day; then we saw her

come out into the sun, denuded, a girl of fifteen, more astonishing than the north star in broad daylight.

Striding angrily, she headed toward the colonist's villa. One hour later, she reappeared, dragging along her moping and crestfallen brother.

I can tell you we were proud of that girl! She made our faces turn red with pleasure.

However, we had no inkling of what was about to happen that evening. Unbeknownst to us, the plot had thickened. We cannot throw a stone at anyone. For each of our destinies is inscribed in the Great Book of the World. Only a thoughtless person believes himself master of his own fate. Despite the severity of our morals, we cannot condemn Ourida, especially since none of us has ever learned the exact circumstances in which the tragedy unfolded. God alone is omniscient.

But we still bear the bruises today. I'll talk about it later, for now I have to tell you the story of the lepers.

THREE DAYS after Omar El Mabrouk's visit, a motorized policeman sheathed in black leather from head to foot, with boots, helmet, and mask, came and pasted a notice on the door of the municipal annex. Urgently summoned, the son of Ali informed us that the notice stipulated that access to public roads was henceforth strictly prohibited for ovines, bovines, caprines, equines, and all other domestic animals, hooved or unhooved, two-legged or four-legged, and that any delinquent beast would be immediately conducted by the police to the communal stable of Sidi Bounemeur, and, unless the owner paid the appropriate fine within three days, said beast would be offered for sale at public auction and sold by full right to the highest bidder for the total amount of his bid plus a tax of ten percent.

Rabah the country constable was astonished to learn from Ali's lips that he was the representative of the powers of law and order and that he was charged with enforcing the new regulation.

"Me?" he exclaimed.

"Absolutely," the son of Ali confirmed.

"But which are the public roads? That narrow, twisting alley?"

Two weeks later, we set eyes again on the abundantly chromized vehicle whose molding seemed intent on multiplying the rays of the sun. We instantly went to awaken

Mohamed, who was having his siesta on a mat in the café. He came dashing out, rubbing his eyes.

Placing one foot on the ground, the prefect snapped at him, "How can you sleep amid this deafening sparrow concert?"

Mohamed was about to shrug when the second question was fired at him: "Well, have you emptied the villas?"

The son of the recruit, who had not yet fully recovered his lucidity, began stammering.

"You people are not going to hoodwink me, I know all of you too well. Behind your mask of submission, you remain wily and devious. You managed to pull some fast ones on the colonists, but that won't work with me. So let's not beat around the bush: either you evacuate those premises within the next few hours or the gendarmes will come and boot your wives and children out with good kicks in their butts."

With his forefinger, he signaled to Mohamed to follow him and he turned his back on us. They walked together for several steps, then the prefect stopped in his tracks. He guffawed spitefully.

"The only alley in this village is even more twisted than your minds. Honestly, can you tell me how we're going to turn this hamlet into an acceptable district seat? 'Now why have they chosen Zitouna?' you're going to ask. After years of dealing with those schemers who govern us, I can perfectly understand their calculations. I was barely out of my teens when I realized I could only benefit from associating with the power brokers of the world. After going underground, I quickly dropped my shit-assed companions and tried to approach those feverish men with shiny eyes. After the independence, I wasn't stupid enough to return to my native village. Instead, I followed the trail of the men who had known where to go from the very outset: they were all heading toward the capital. You people thought I was dead, but I was lounging around in a luxurious residence in the city. I lived there without a twinge of remorse. I had asked for an ambassadorship and, while waiting for my appointment, I drew a colossal salary for a position flimsier than the superstitions that clog up your minds. Director general of God knows what—I never found out. My minister had known me in the maquis and he felt no desire whatsoever to get to know me any better. He never thought of allocating an office for me, and I never thought of requesting one. On the other hand, I made sure to demand the official automobile that I was entitled to. Jet-black and decked out with shiny moldings. Its soft and easy seats welcomed me as gently as a loving woman. All I had to do was spend an hour driving through the wind with all the windows down, with no schedule or destination—and that was enough to make up for all my hard years of marching my feet off in the jebels (mountains). That shithead of a superior: he sent me the car with an official chauffeur. The guy had also been in the underground, and he couldn't figure out why he should be under my orders and not the other way round, he couldn't figure out why I was the director and he an employee on the bottom rung. He told me that he and I were both illiterates who had sprung from the same soil and gone off at the same time to do some shooting in the mountains. And so, he insisted, can you explain this to me? Since I had no desire to drag that bellyacher along everywhere, I confiscated his keys and told him to go cultivate his resentments and his memories somewhere else.

"And thus, while waiting for my ambassadorship year after year, I spent my mornings dozing, my afternoons looking for sex, and my nights drinking and fornicating. God forgive me, but I took more women to bed than there are olive trees in your fields. You can't imagine how many broads out there are addicted to the smell of power. They swarm around every mover and shaker. They jostle about at every reception, each woman more ravishing than the next. Most of them are drawn by luxury and lavishness, as if they were trying to wreak vengeance for some obscure and distant past filled with austerity and deprivation. But the most perverse and most fascinating ones are sensitive only to the charisma of those men who are so certain of their power that they pretend to hide it. These women are haughty and Machiavellian. They have a knack for docking at the most hostile shores, beleaguering fortresses that are reputed to be invincible. Eventually they cast their spell, making you totally dependent on them, before leading you from renunciation to renunciation, from betrayal to betrayal, until you surrender so unconditionally that you sacrifice advantages and privileges, career, wife, and children, honor and dignity, not to mention your convictions. I took that road. It's tragic but irresistible. You know me: I can't see beyond the tip of my penis. In my teens, I even took up with that horror Suzanne, you must remember. Yet I had a fine future ahead of me. At worst, I would have become a colonel without an army, commanding nothing but my pretorian guard, letting them cool their heels outside my office from dawn till dusk.

"My vice wrecked my career. That's why I'm stuck in this goddamn, godforsaken village today. Zitouna, the district seat! What a riot! I could laugh till I choke!

"Why did they pick Zitouna? you'll keep asking me. I think I can explain the motives of those sly dogs in the capital. They preferred not to choose between two cities of equal importance, which, however, have been deadly rivals since the dawn of time. Our traditions of compromise always want us to slice the pear into even halves. So they tried to find a place exactly equidistant between those two competing centers. And this place was Zitouna. My native village. Fucking shit! Since my name was clogging up their files, they hit on the ingenious idea of naming me prefect. They must be having a good laugh today, in the coolness of their air-conditioned offices, picturing me sweating like a pig in this Gehenna.

"I'm going to raze all the houses on top, all the houses at the bottom, and replace them with tall, rectilinear apartment buildings, and their façades will be whiter than the intimate parts of your women. You'll live there on top of one another and you'll pay rents more precious than the smile of your first baby."

The son of Messaoud listened wordlessly.

"I take great pleasure in informing you that since Zitouna has become *ipso facto* an entirely separate parish, I have appointed you its mayor by virtue of the powers invested in me. Here is the order," he added, producing a document from his pocket. "You can go and trumpet it around to your constituents, change the stamp that you lug around in your pocket, and start building your dreams of power. The imam will no longer be able to withhold his virgin's vagina from your sons. Quite the contrary: he'll be honored having his daughter enter the family of the highest V.I.P. in the village. For needless to say, your djemaa is hereby automatically disbanded. You will warn the members of that august assembly that any meeting of that body is henceforth illegal. We cannot allow two decision-making entities to coexist."

"But who's going to settle conflicts between the inhabitants?"

"You, and you alone. You'll have the law and the police on your side. Plus my prudent advice. Don't forget that the first time my balls start to itch, I'll kick you out with another decree. Then again, if you retain my lessons, you won't even have to pretend to campaign in the next elections. I'll distribute magic ballot boxes throughout the parish territory, and your name will ineluctably come out no matter what name is on the ballots that the voters insert. Your first decision as mayor of Zitouna will be to prohibit any oil industry anywhere in the district."

"I don't understand."

"That mill was acquired by the sweat of my father's brow, and he spent most of his life plowing the neighbors' fields while his grandfather profited from his labors. The clubfoot blithely inherited the press, whereas, in all fairness, it should have passed on to me. We're going to shut it down."

"But he's your adoptive father."

"Exactly. I haven't forgotten anything he put me through. I just don't happen to have a very forgiving nature. I'm going to make that bastard pay for the whole backlog of abuse and punishment."

"But how are we supposed to get oil?"

"I'll send you whole truckloads of colza oil that will be clearer than your vision of the happy valley, blonder than the blondest of dunes, produced in factories more terrifying than the ocean monsters in your fairy tales, and it will come to you, ready for consumption, in beautiful plastic drums. Believe me, you won't lose anything in the exchange."

Then, turning toward us, Omar El Mabrouk loudly declared, "I have some good news to announce: you will soon be finding the brothers and cousins who have left you. I know that it will be a great joy for you."

None of us understood what he meant until the following Friday, at the end of the great noon prayer.

First there was a dull rumble. Echoed and amplified by the surrounding mountains, the monstrous roar seemed to flood in from all sides. It recalled the war days, when the German bombardiers dawdled through the air, hunting for

American bases. So we looked up at the sky. But they came from the slope: two motorcycle policemen with flashing lights, followed by a convoy of immense trucks sporting more wheels than a caterpillar has feet. They lined up next to the eucalyptus forest. The cops and the drivers seemed hurried if not jumpy. You would have thought they were scared of our children, who began clustering around them. They exchanged some furtive signs, then the tips of the trucks went up and everything came crashing to the ground. Ashamed, the vehicles did a U-turn and fled.

The wretched odds and ends lay on the ground, indecently exposed to rubberneckers. Battered mattresses, bundles of linen wrapped in sheets, a few aluminum utensils, a gaudy scattering of plastic objects.

Next, two buses showed up, bringing back the outlaws. Each of them was clutching his most fragile if not most precious possession in his arms: a radio, a coffee grinder, a camera, a tea service, a few Koranic verses in a frame. They climbed out slowly. There were the twins, Méziane and Améziane, the blacksmith's oldest son with his widened mouth and graying hair, and Mokhtar, who had once carried himself so proudly and was now stooped, and Mohamed's brother, and the man with six fingers, and all the other men who had once left us.

They plodded toward us with lowered heads, abashed and contrite, as if they had committed the seven deadly sins. With heavy hearts and outstretched arms, we walked toward them, our imam in the lead. People hugged for a long time. Then our sheik told them, "Welcome back. You are the sons of our tribe, you are at home here."

They were astonished by our brotherly reception. They hadn't expected it. We now witnessed some poignant scenes: not only the women and children, but also the highly virile men began weeping shamelessly.

"We've been turned away everywhere, we've encountered nothing but hostility and rejection wherever we've gone."

We organized a great banquet in their honor, and the most impoverished man in the village insisted on sacrificing a goat.

At teatime, the most eloquent among us told them, "Our memories have always kept alive every instant of each of your departures, and our hearts have never stopped feeling the void of your absence. We knew that you did not leave us with gaiety in your hearts. How can anyone forbid those who have lost everything to hope for a more endurable future? The destiny of each one of us is written in the Great Book. But without daring to say anything to you, we sensed that even if you prospered down there, in the cities of the plain, you would have to endure far greater misfortunes. No man can live happily outside his own country."

Drying their tears, the most deeply affected among them recounted their adventures.

"They accused us of every evil. They told us that we were the source of all the illnesses ravaging the city: the swarming streets, the hopelessly empty shop stalls, the endless trafficking in the harbors, and the overcrowded prisons and hospitals, the always-tiny schools, the buses gasping under the overload of passengers, the water more rare than in the sands of the desert, the sewers vomiting into the streets, the proliferating rats, the cats gone mad, the mosquitoes indifferent to insecticides. They assured us that it was our fault that the rain refused to fall or else flooded the sidewalks, that the sun pouted behind the mountains, the price of oil had stopped rising, the workers stopped working, the sweepers stopped sweeping. They made us suffer the worst humiliations. Morning and evening, evening and morning, arrogant policemen came to check on our number and our sex, as if, in the meantime, we might have increased one and changed the other. Our children were expelled from the schools, our sick from the hospitals, our workers from the factories. The municipal registration offices were closed to our newborn and our dead, and the administrations ignored us. Little by little, they ordered us to stop doing laundry, cooking, stocking up on water, relieving ourselves, having our wives, and then going out in the daylight. We felt excluded from the community of the Prophet. Finally, they revealed to us the nature of the illness that had stricken us."

Other outcasts went on: "We were told we had leprosy. We then went together to the baths, where each of us in turn had his body examined by the others. As meticulous as we were, we could detect no chancre. Our skins were perfectly clear. But, refusing to trust our eyes, we consulted the most famous healers, the most expert physicians. None of them discovered even the slightest sign of an ailment in us. We communicated our perplexity to those who had announced our disease to us.

" 'No use torturing yourselves,' they said, 'it's a special form of leprosy. Not only is it invisible, but it is impossible to track down with traditional methods.'

" 'But what do you base your diagnosis on?'

" 'Our deep-seated conviction. Look at the façades of the buildings in front of you. They're already contaminated, and your disease might spread to the entire city. We are particularly concerned about the most shaded districts, the homes of people with sensitive souls and delicate bodies. But you needn't worry, we've taken the matter in hand. And we've decided to let you benefit gratis from the most tried-and-tested prophylactic treatment. To restore your health, you'll have to leave the atmosphere of the cities and return to the healthy peaks of your native mountains. That is your only chance of salvation. Trust us, we have taken care of everything.'

"And that Friday, armed policemen in battle-dress stormed and captured our shantytown, benefiting, as in a real battle, from the surprise and swiftness of the maneuver. They made us rush out of our shacks, they counted us off once again, they dumped our belongings into the waiting trucks, and then the bulldozers charged forward with low-ered shovels and, in the twinkling of an eye, they knocked down our plywood and sheet-metal hovels. At sunrise, our neighbors discovered a leveled terrain. Their wives let out whoops of joy."

Our imam replied, "We believe in Allah and his Apostle, but not in the poppycock of our remote leaders. They have learned to govern with lies and double-dealing and they imagine they can pull the wool over our eyes. But the truth of it is: they are fooling no one but themselves. They have fed us so many fables that they no longer know where the sun comes up or what the first names of their children are, they don't know the color of the sky or the time of day. You are wrong to credit anything they tell you. Here, among your brethren, you will recover your spiritual health. During your absence, we have scrupulously watched over the lands and goods that you have left behind, as well as over your daughters who were given in marriage. You will settle under the eucalyptuses, and as of tomorrow, we will help you rebuild your ruined houses and work your abandoned fields."

The eldest of the lepers proved worthy of our trust and tried to adapt to their new life-style. But we realized that the minds of their adolescents had been thoroughly perverted. They had forgotten all our customs and traditions, and their behavior was shocking. They refused to participate in the reconstruction of their own homes and they refused, even

more categorically, to work the soil. They preferred spending their days going and coming, unabashedly and indis-
creetly reveling in violent and unseemly music. We have
always distrusted music-lovers and poets. They are slug-
gards. They shrink from honest labor and they are always
willing to succumb to the most dangerous bents. We sys-
tematically discourage such propensities among our young
people in order to orient them toward the psalmody of the
Koran. But the sons of the lepers seemed to delight in those
tendencies. Their attitudes were truly scandalous. They
smoked or chewed tobacco in front of their fathers, they had
the nerve to ask them for money to spend on trifles, they
entered the courtyards of houses without resonantly cough-
ing to announce themselves. It soon dawned on us that their
tricks to make contact with our virgins were aimed purely
at pleasure, for these young whippersnappers did not wish
to marry. However, our aggressively virtuous maidens, who
caught on quickly, made short shrift of them and sent them
packing with their tails between their legs.

"Where are the streets where anything is bought and
sold, the movie theaters with seductive posters, the opulent
pastry shops, those mobbed buses where you can squeeze
against buttocks that are softer than the memory of my first
love, those chilly bars that sell and serve beer with overflow-
ing foam, and all those beautiful girls who pass back and
forth, going to work, shopping, wiggling their hips, shriek-
ing with laughter, appearing to grow lovelier in the spring,
then stripping down on the hot sand in the summer and
offering their sore breasts to the embrace of the surf? Here,
all you see is scrofulous fig trees and cantankerous goats.
What are we doing here?"

A few weeks later, several of the youths had disappeared.
When asked about them, their fathers shrugged their shoulders. We were puzzled by their ignorance and unconcern.

"Where have they gone? Aren't you worried?"

"Those boys are unhappy," they replied. "We shouldn't judge them too severely. When we headed into exile, we believed we were concerned about their future, but we were concerned only about ourselves. We were thoughtless. We didn't realize what was awaiting them. They were born and raised in the shantytown, across from huge apartment buildings that challenged them with their height. Five short yards separating two universes. None of them ever managed to cross the gap. As children, they became aware of the difference; as adolescents, they could no longer endure it. Long before we were told, they knew they were stricken with that invisible and insidious disease that ultimately forced us to return. They lived on temptations and frustrated desires. At night, they dreamt, leaning against the wall, gazing up at the high, indecently lit windows that showed them people of their own age, sexes mingling, dancing, eating, drinking, laughing. They noticed the *tête-à-têtes*, the confidences, the caresses, the furtive kisses. In the daytime, they dreamed of those leather jackets and foreign trousers that we could not afford to buy them. Yes, they simply wanted to be like the others. That was their way of coddling themselves. And so a few of them began lining up at supermarkets to buy scarce goods and resell them in the street; others went down to the harbor with its endless trafficking to buy and sell contraband. Sometimes a police raid would clean the streets of those illegal peddlers, and they would spend one or two whole days in the lockup. As soon as they were released, they would go back to their peddling. Then they were taken to prison, where they were bound to establish useful contacts. As a result, they would vanish more and more often, for longer and longer periods. We got used to it. Yes, those children are very unhappy, excluded down there, and maladjusted up here."

After a while, however, they returned in handcuffs, accompanied by gendarmes. And once again they went down to the city, and once again they were brought back, until the day that a furious Omar El Mabrouk landed here.

"You have to learn to keep a tight hand on your little brats. We've already explained about how their presence endangers innocent city dwellers. Those children are minors and thus they are under parental protection. You are responsible for them. From now on, if any child runs away, his father will have to pay a huge fine."

Before leaving, he added, "Some men will be visiting you soon. I hope you receive them with the consideration that my future colleagues deserve."

AND THUS, during the next few days, there were several brief forays by automobilists. They prudently halted several hundred yards from the fig-tree square. The lowered car window revealed a flabbergasted gape. Very soon, the car did a U-turn and vanished. We sensed how horrified those enlighteners were at the thought of settling in Zitouna. Omar El Mabrouk deployed all his oratorical skills trying to convince them.

"Don't worry," he told them, "trust me, I've thought of everything."

He promised to send away to Canada, that never-never land, for villas especially for them: with aluminum roofs and cardboard walls, but so well-crafted that the metal would be lighter than the breath of my lastborn and the cardboard harder than our heads. He specified that these villas would all be equipped with those apparatuses that blow cold in summer and hot in winter, not to mention furniture of imitation wood, and, as a signal favor, those boxes that make you laugh and cry, and of which they knew they had become ardent and inveterate admirers, as with all those gadgets that stealthily undermined the foundations of wisdom and faith.

"I'll have a swimming pool dug as deep as you like in front of every home. At the end of each day, you can dive

in and drown your professional and family cares and watch
your children frolicking there or some tender Venus who
will know how to thank you later that night. Likewise, I'll
set up a special tax-free cooperative to sell you all brands of
whiskey and the rarest liquors, a hundred varieties of cheese,
those with the firm consistence of the breast of a barely
nubile virgin, those with the softness of desired lips, those
that melt like my heart at the smile of my firstborn. You
won't have to suffer from the chaos of the peasants. I'll
surround your houses with a high wall protected by an
electric fence. Furthermore, I am authorized to pay you
phenomenal salaries, most of which you will put by, and
each of you will be flown abroad once every four months,
gratis, to the country of your choice, with all expenses paid.
You can take along the women whose glances, smiles, or
buttocks haunt your nights, or you can simply rifle those
foreign stores with their cheap profusion. For your children,
we will set up a school from the same faraway country, state
of the art, in perfect working order, and so spic-and-span
that it will look like a comic strip, plus school mistresses
purchased at the same time as the furniture and with diapha-
nous cheeks that will inspire the dreams of all the mousta-
chioed men for miles around."

We couldn't tell whether Omar El Mabrouk managed to
tempt his audience. At any rate, we had a lull of several
months. The prefect lay low, the automobilists no longer
came to show us their stupefied faces, the sons of the lepers
soft-pedaled the utterances of their melancholy. We felt we
had regained our routine and our serenity.

Only Mohamed's life was topsy-turvy. He waffled for a
long time before making up his mind to issue his first municipal edict. One morning, he discreetly arrived at the office
of Ali son of Ali.

"You're the only one who knows the language of the

Roumis. So you can compose the text. I'll have it typed up by the public scribe in Sidi Bounemeur."

"I'm opposed to your plan."

"I'm asking for your help, not your advice."

"People might think I'm an accomplice to your wire-pulling."

"You can't refuse. This is a requisition that I'm formulating for you in my capacity as mayor."

"Goodness, you're a fast learner."

Instructed by the prefect's precedent, Mohamed ordered the country constable to enforce his edict. Because of their family ties, Rabah allowed himself a certain familiarity with the mayor.

"You're doing something awfully dumb."

"That's my business."

"In that case, go and tell him yourself. You know very well he's my brother-in-law."

"The law is the same for everyone. You have to submit to your duty."

Sick at heart, Rabah went to tell Aïssa the oil-presser that he was ordered to cease his activity.

"I know that the decision comes from the man who grew up among my children. That man is a mad dog. He bites anything within reach. I'm convinced that you and Mohamed are not involved. But you can't keep playing both sides of the fence. You're apostates and you will live like apostates."

Aïssa looked away and contemplated his machine.

"I was just preparing for the next harvest."

He shook his head for a long time.

"I still have a small reserve of oil, over there in the corner. I advise you to take a few containers. I wouldn't want my sister's children to suffer the consequences of your stupidity."

* * *

On a day like any other, long before the dawn prayer, we were awakened by such a dreadful boom that we thought the favorable wrath of heaven was exploding. But once we got outdoors, we saw that no cloud was threatening our still-undone turbans. So then we figured that a new contingent of lepers had arrived, ten times larger than the first, to judge by the racket.

"Have they decided to rid the cities of their jobless, homeless, penniless? Can't they stand the sight of filth, poverty, destitution? Are they the ones who are suffering? Now who's going to pick up the greasy garbage, unchoke the stinking sewers, unload the cargoes from the ships?"

We were wrong. These were not lepers.

More numerous than the stars in the sky, more uproarious than a herd of raging camels, the foreigners disembarked in our village without prior warning. Driven by tiny manikins, their trucks were ten times more enormous than those that had carried the lepers. After laboring up the slope, they aimed their terrifying muzzles, one after the other. Each of them was carrying a ready-made house on its back. Since they had so little space, the road monsters did not hesitate to beleaguer our fields, settling down as in a conquered land. They toiled forward, lumbered back, maneuvered, honked like there was no tomorrow, heedless of the disorder they were sowing. Massed on the fig-tree square, we patiently waited for the chief of the midgets to come and wish us peace and give us the reasons for their arrival.

Our waiting was useless. At sunrise, the invaders sat down by their trucks and began eating breakfast. Outraged by their conduct, we instantly went to fetch our mayor.

"Who are they? Where do they come from? What do they want?"

"Let's not get excited," he replied. "I suggest that we first go to my café and brew a nice hot tea. It's on the house."

Once each of us was holding his burning glass, the first accusation was launched. "This is a new initiative of Omar El Mabrouk, and you've got a finger in the pie."

The mayor flatly denied it.

"It's a *fait accompli*. What do you intend to do?"

"We have to reflect."

"We can't allow those intruders to occupy our fields like this. Not to mention that their iron monsters have scattered panic among our animals. Listen to the bleating of our goats."

"The prefect is certainly going to come and furnish some useful explanations. We have to wait for him."

"What if he doesn't show up?"

"He is the head authority not only for Zitouna, but for all the villages around here and throughout the countryside. We have to respect his position."

"I tell you: We won't see hide nor hair of him. He can't be too proud of his sneaky tricks, and he's probably even less eager to come and face our legitimate anger."

We finally gave in to the mayor. But the sun was starting to sink, and none of the children who had been sent out to watch for the appearance of the black automobile had returned. Utterly indifferent to our existence, the foreigners were still bustling among the trucks.

"They have no intention of leaving," the observers noted.

"Well?" asked the most impatient.

Thus challenged, Mohamed made a skeptical face.

"I'm going to ask our constable to talk to them."

"You know very well that despite his uniform, Rabah is a shrinking violet. He'll scamper off at the first beep."

"What else can we do?"

"You are our representative and the leader of the parish. You have to go and talk to them."

"But I don't speak their language. The son of Ali is the only one who's attended the school of the Roumis."

Georgeaud interrupted in a categorical tone of voice:

"Those people don't speak the language of the French or the Germans. They use an even stranger jargon."

"Is there anyone here who knows the language of these foreigners?" the mayor asked.

A pointless question. Mohamed knew perfectly well that we experienced our language as a rampart and that we hadn't even taken the trouble to learn the language of the Roumis, even though they had remained in our land for a long time. The same was true of Georgeaud, even though he had remained in their land for a long time. Likewise, we had never admitted to understanding the language of the men of the cold, who, nevertheless, use the words of the Koran.

"What do you suggest?" the mayor said.

"They're the ones who've come here, it's up to them to use the language of our country."

"You think so? Yet our tongue is reputed to be so rich and so subtle that many natives prove incapable of mastering it. That's why we so greatly admire our ancient poets. These foreigners couldn't even imitate our sonorities."

"We know they're insatiably curious and willing to study anything in the world, including things that don't concern them at all. They're bound to have an interpreter."

The imam, who had been holding his peace, went up to the municipal official. We instantly fell silent.

"Your forebears were outlaws who were welcomed by our tribe and admitted into its bosom. And they rapidly became part of us. You know very well that we have never balked at giving you our virgins. The proof is that your son will soon be marrying my youngest daughter. The behavior of your fathers never led us to regret our decision. Today, you have become our administrative leader and you have to show that you are worthy of the trust we have placed in your family."

Mohamed took the blacksmith's youngest son to a corner and conversed with him in a low voice.

"You really saw these foreigners up close?"

"I was perched on a eucalyptus."

"Are they really as small as we're told?"

"The smallest wheel on their engines is twice their size, and you could lodge a hundred of those dwarves in a single one of the houses they're transporting."

Mohamed threw out his chest and came back to us.

"Okay," he exclaimed, "I'll go and see them. As soon as we perform our religious duties. I'll take along the constable as the representative of the police. You never can tell. It may be necessary to use force."

The imam nodded briskly, and we followed him into the prayer room. After the service, our mayor went home to don his official burnoose. Then he went to the barber and had his moustache trimmed imposingly before taking down the old rifle he had inherited from his great-grandfather. He spent a long time harnessing his mule. Then, jumping into the saddle, he harangued his admiring constituents.

"In the past, the cruel winds of adversity blasted over us repeatedly. We then experienced the bruises of reality and the lengthy nights of confusion. But we have always survived. Today, we will again bear up. If I do not return, then let me entrust my children to the most generous among you and the leadership of our community to the wisest. Let me remind you that you are all witnesses to the fact that the imam has agreed to give his youngest daughter to my son."

He spoke; then, after a noble salute, he began to advance.

Turning away, he told the constable, "Follow me only at a good distance. This could get dangerous."

MASSED ON THE fig-tree square, the populace was awaiting the return of its envoys. We were dumbfounded to see them shuffling back, unarmed, with a hangdog look, dragging their unsaddled mule by its bridle.

We started trembling and invoking the power of Allah, for our collective memory had kept alive the tales of ancient times when our fathers were forced to pay the price of wasted time. History is spiteful, as was the lieutenant with the curled-up moustache who led the detachment of helmeted soldiers. From his high horse, he ordered the enumeration of all males of a fighting age (five years and older, in his eyes), the confiscation of the same number of chargers, all the rifles, as well as stores of powder and bullets, and the payment, within a month, of cereals, cattle, gold, and silver as a war tribute calculated in proportion to the number of warriors in the tribe.

Thus their grain reserves melted, and their herds were scattered. They learned that all the land in the happy valley was sequestered, that they had to part with one half of the lands that they were occupying without permission; for those lands, by the document of surrender, had become the property of the Empire. The surveyor's alidade would be coming to mark off their billeting area and the price to be paid in cereals, gold, and silver. Next, the hakem, the military judge, announced that they were not allowed to travel, and that they would be held collectively responsible and be collectively punished for even the slightest disturbance in the region. Pulling a sheet of paper from his pocket, he read them the decree that appointed the principal chiefs of the tribe to the office of caïd in places remote from, and unknown to, them. This spelled exile for Omar ben Hassan, the noblest of the nobles, and Mabrouk ibn Tofaïl, the eldest son of the holy founder, and Ahmed Er Rihani, chief of the most important çof (regiment) of the tribe, and so many others as well. Finally, the officer informed them that all the commanders of goums were to be interned until further notice and that they had to surrender to him in order to be taken to the military barracks.

We were told that Ibn Abdelmalek then stepped forward.

He was the most gallant of the gallant, the most cunning of the cunning, always the first to lead a charge and the last to cover the retreat, with his red burnoose flapping in the wind. His scimitar had sliced through so many infidel necks that legend calls him the heir to Ali, the invincible companion of the Prophet.

Upon seeing him approach, the interpreter couldn't help drawing back.

Straightening his torso, Ibn Abdelmalek addressed the horseman, "This is the land of our fathers and our fathers' fathers, who dwelled here long before the Tiding and long before the arrival of the Roums. We have always risen up to combat the invader no matter where he came from. We have often repulsed him, he has sometimes dominated us. As victors, we have never outraged the dignity of our adversaries, and as losers, we have never had to suffer from a lack of consideration. As a warrior, I was born to fight, and your troops are well aware that my sword is more redoubtable than a hundred of your ancient rifles. Our ranks have been decimated, not by your bravery, but by those chassepots, which do not have to be reloaded. The glory belongs not to your armies but to your inventors. Since I have been beaten today, I accept death, which delivers, but not imprisonment, which debases. If you refuse to kill me on the spot, then I will draw my scimitar, swoop down upon you, and, within the twinkling of an eye, I will have sliced through a dozen necks."

He was killed.

But we knew that those times and their methods were gone, that the invaders had stored their ravaging cannon, their obstinate tanks, and their invincible planes in their overseas depots, that henceforth they would be content to blithely flood the cities of our country with apparatuses that reproduce voices and shapes, despite the Prophet's prohibition, and which sap the minds of those who truckle to them.

Thus, we failed to understand why they had humiliated our messenger, who was nevertheless smiling as he came back.

After getting rid of the swarm of brats harassing them, the adult male population, following its leader, settled down on the mats diligently laid out by courtesy of Mohamed's eldest son. And, once the tea was served, our emissary launched into a blow-by-blow description of his encounter with the foreigners.

After riding up to them on his mule, he said:

"The leader of the natives wishes to speak with the leader of the foreigners. If you are in the habit of living like barbarians, without law or leader, you will designate the man most worthy to represent you, in honor and nobility. Tell him that he will have to come with his face uncovered."

The blacksmith's youngest son asked him:

"Do they come from the land of the dwarves?"

"Actually, once they climb down from their machines, they recover their normal size. Our tales have often noted such phenomena."

The foreigners did have an interpreter, but he spoke only the language of the Koran, having learned it, no doubt, from books more rigorous than the phrases he was uttering. They couldn't believe we were using a different language. For an instant, Mohamed was tempted to summon the blacksmith's youngest boy, who had garnered all the known verses of the Koran; indeed, after the invasion of that scatter-brain of a teacher, he had wanted to go to the French school in Sidi Bounemeur to wear out the seat of his pants and his father's savings. However, the boy proved more skillful at handling a slingshot than the sacred tongue. He flunked his courses and broke the windows of the school. They expelled him.

Our mayor felt that the long meetings of the Party cell had sufficiently initiated him into the niceties of the language of the cold-dwellers.

That is to say, the discussion proved laborious and was riddled with misunderstandings and peculiarities.

"We have not learned to love the strangers. Misfortune always arrives with them. What are you doing here?"

They showed him a thick document.

"This."

"I don't understand. But I must warn you that we will not be taken advantage of. If necessary, we will summon a child of our village who worked for a long time in the cold land and who has recently become head not only of this village but also of the entire surrounding countryside as far as your eyes can see. He is big, very powerful, and you ought to be afraid of his anger."

"We too come from the land of cold."

"What do you mean?"

"For six months of the year, the high, white snow covers the ground. In the cold, the ears freeze, the nose drips, the cheeks sparkle, the eyes tear."

"I meant the places that are cold despite the blazing sun."

"We don't understand."

"Do we have to describe the sanctuary of the loftiest district of the city of cities, at the summit of the highest of the apartment buildings, the dwellings of men who are so powerful that their slightest frown causes earthquakes in all countries, men so dreadful that they intimidate the rays of the sun, which are afraid to darken the translucence of their cheeks. Thus, their faces have nothing but the cadaverous pallor of power. Omar El Mabrouk is one of them."

"He's the one we signed the contract with."

"Omar El Mabrouk?"

"Precisely. And since we've greased all the necessary palms, we hope we can get to work very quickly."

"Your trucks have invaded our fields, terrified our animals, disturbed the sleep of the birds in our eucalyptuses, shaken the newly built shacks of the lepers."

"Men and beasts have to clear out from these places so our vehicles can unload their freight. But we're worried about those sick people being so close by. There's no mention of that in the contract."

After gulping down another mouthful from his glass, Mohamed told us that he had declared.

"Don't worry, we know how to keep our diseases to ourselves and keep our deepest bruises a secret. Actually, these poor people are affected only by an optical illusion provoked by the curiosity of foreign photographers who thoughtlessly have a good standing in the capital. They are suffering only in their dignity and they will heal when their blindness is over."

"We'll take the precaution of vaccinating our personnel.

An additional clause will have to be added to the contract to cover this additional cost."

Our indignant spokesman explained to them that we could not refuse asylum or fraternal compassion to these dishonored men who had come to seek the merciful shade of our huge trees in order to hide the sores they were said to be carrying and whose presence they had not managed to ascertain despite all their examinations. Upon returning to our village, they had, as a matter of duty, immersed themselves in baths in which eucalyptus leaves, with their well-known antiseptic virtues, had been steeping for a long time. Our interpreter added that our collective wisdom was acquainted with the harshness of exile.

"The people of our tribe were always sick at heart watching their sons leave. There were those who, refusing to live under the infidel yoke, emigrated to Islamic soil; those who, upon descending victorious from the mountains, believed they could rediscover the valley of dahlias and nightingales; those who, egged on by hunger, crossed the sea or went to the cities of the plain, beyond the great river and beyond the railroad. And we have always kept hoping they would return from exile, as arrogant richlings or bitter unfortunates."

After a pause, the orator added, "You have to ignore their imaginary wounds and train yourselves in our indulgent blindness. Since a son of this village has given you his word, we will welcome you as brothers if you know how to merit our trust. We advise you against isolating yourselves and living in a horde as you are used to doing. Furthermore, in my capacity as mayor, I must inform you that it is illegal to eat the stray cats and dogs of the area as is, supposedly, your custom. We do not permit those barbarous customs."

That was the speech that our negotiator claimed to have given. We were fired by the eloquence and nobility of his diction despite the constable's frequent attempts at correcting him. However, our annoyed gestures made it clear to the constable that the artistic harmony of a narrative could accommodate a little stretching of the exact truth and that, although anything but gullible, we preferred the finery and bedizenment of the imagination to the austere nakedness of reality.

Finally, the question that was racking us was asked.

"Why did they confiscate your rifle and your saddle?"

Our café owner gratified us with a broad smile.

"I know what you might have been fearing."

He now told us that throughout the conversation, the leader of the foreigners had kept his eyes glued to the rifle resting on his lap. His gaze became so intense that our hero felt it was necessary to reassure his interlocutor.

"Don't worry, we are not going to shoot you or cut off your nice blond heads. Our ancestral defeat forced us to place our antiquated combativeness on the shelf of nostalgia. Upon recovering its sovereignty, our country felt it had to open up to the world. It agreed to have dealings with men who are as pale as you and who rank profit above honor. Thus our government exchanges our beautiful wheat for evil apparatuses of chrome-plated metal, for arrogant knowledge, and for proletarian sweat. We have already had to experience your efficiency and we deplore our vulnerability. We welcome you with the bitter awareness that you will profit from our hospitality to pervert our universe. You will benefit from our obsolete values and, ridiculing our scruples, you will pocket your dollars. You may be ruthlessly triumphant today, but, if you wish to regain your souls, you must double back along the road of generous humanity that has left us helpless. From our defeat and self-denial we have forged a morality that helps us to live on a higher level than your comfort."

However, the foreigner's lustful stare remained focused on the chiseled mother-of-pearl butt of Mohamed's heirloom rifle.

"Since he acted indifferent to the beauty of my harangue, I dickered with him for a long time and finally palmed off my blunderbuss for a radio that's so powerful it can capture the voices of countries as far away as the one they come from. I swapped the leather saddle with the silver embroidery for a state-of-the-art percolator that'll be delivered within six months. Isn't that a windfall!"

FOR THE CORNERSTONE ceremony, Omar El Mabrouk invited a personnage whose position was so lofty that his feet could not reach the ground. They therefore had to roll out a carpet thick enough for him to agree to risk setting foot here. During the days leading up the visit, we saw the prefect arriving early every morning, hustling and bustling more feverishly than a rutting buck. He was accompanied by people so grave and so important that we thought they had to bear the weight of the sky. Facing their severe or skeptical glares, Omar El Mabrouk promised, assured, reassured.

We observed this agitation from our fig-tree square, but never interfered, except when they tried to move the old lawyer. This obdurate defender of all lost causes had been exiled twice to our region.

The first time, quite a while back, during that troubled period of the war, he stepped out of a police vehicle and was handed over to the French military officer who had been installed here. We were astonished to note that the lieutenant, who acted haughty and scornful toward us, showed a mixture of fear and respect toward this frail manikin, who was awkward in his movements, embarrassed about his body, and so unsteady on his feet that he could have been knocked to the ground by a child's shove. For a long time, we kept wondering what this fragile city boy was doing here. Cautiously, we scrutinized him from a distance, commenting lengthily on anything he did. He was lodged at the villa requisitioned by the officer and he ate at his table. We could easily have mistaken him for one of those strange Roumis, half-lunatic, half-learned, who sometimes came here for several weeks to watch us live. But this man could not take a step without the lieutenant's stooge, a harki named Onion-Head, whose laugh, like that of a sadistic moron, cleared a path for him. Every morning, the manikin came and had his tea at Mohamed's café. Sipping his beverage, he sat in a corner, silent and reserved, ignoring the rowdy companionship of his bald watchdog. Sometimes we would see the lawyer taking long walks with the officer. On the morning of Aïd, at prayer time, we were astonished to see him arrive alone and join us. At the end of the service, the imam invited him to share our meal. He accepted gladly. After the couscous, during tea, we lapsed into silence. Civility forbids questioning a guest. But he sensed the curiosity shining in our attentive eyes.

"You must be wondering about the reasons for my presence in this village. The colonial authorities have ordered me to reside here."

Since we failed to understand, he explained that he was a semi-prisoner. We gaped at him, disconcerted—and to think we had assumed that the joking idiot was assigned to protect him, not guard him.

"The Roumis have become so powerful that they don't even fear God, and yet they're scared of you?"

When he began speaking, we were surprised by his perfect mastery of our language. But about all, we discovered the passion animating that sickly body and the danger represented by this man's secure speech and calm conviction. We also thought about what the mountebank had predicted.

Ordinarily, the adolescents were uninterested in our debates and walked out after their last mouthful. But that day, they remained.

"Why have you waited so long to come to us?" a young man asked him.

"I wasn't allowed. Today, on the occasion of Aïd, I received special authorization."

Afterwards, the exile wanted to visit the mausoleum of our saint. He was delighted to discover the library. He asked if he could consult the books.

"These volumes of profane speculation and curiosity are forbidden," the imam replied. "No one can have access to them."

Our guest then told us that the time had come to rediscover memory in order to attain the future. Although unconvinced, the imam nevertheless handed him the keys. The man obtained permission from the French military officer to spend two hours a day in the sanctuary. A few adolescents surreptitiously joined him here, and the reading sessions quickly turned into political harangues. This was not to our liking, but none of us dared interfere.

Greedily inhaling the dust of the disarranged manuscripts, the youths peppered the exile with questions.

"Do you believe that we will ever rediscover the valley of sagebrush and turtledoves?"

Tirelessly, the manikin explained, detailed, illustrated, initiated, developed, insisted, resumed. At the end of these debates, his listeners returned to us as if inwardly illuminated.

Omar El Mabrouk was one of them.

Several weeks later, most of them disappeared into the night. When the officer found out, he had a fit. The lawyer was no longer allowed to approach or even greet any of us.

* * *

Yes, now I'm going to tell you what happened to Ourida, the sister whom Omar El Mabrouk seemed to have completely forgotten. I must warn you that the memory of those events is still very painful for me.

After the group of adolescents took off for the maquis, we saw Onion-Head arriving on the fig-tree square, emitting a volley of his mirth. He was accompanied by two henchmen armed with rifles. The mission that the lieutenant had just assigned him lifted him to the acme of jubilation. He joyfully ordered his underlings to flush out the wanted men no matter where they were, and to bring them back to the agora with rifles in their ribs. Soon they were assembled near the square where we were standing. We noticed that they included the fathers and brothers of those who had linked up with the men of the night. After contemplating them for a long time, Onion-Head announced between a couple of guffaws, "I'm missing two."

"You, and you," he said, indecently pointing his forefinger at two of the onlookers. "Stand up. Go join your buddies!"

The group was handed over to a pair of harkis, who conducted them to the French military annex. But the sergeant stayed put and kept cackling defiantly at us. The expression of his glee made his protuberant belly quake.

"There's one more person I have to get," he said suavely.

And turning his back on us, he vanished into an alley. He returned several moments later, dragging Ourida by the arm; she struggled like a she-devil while Aïssa's wife kept punching and berating the callous Cerberus. The indignant crowd got up and began surrounding the satyr.

"Leave that girl alone, bastard!"

Without releasing Ourida's wrist, the man pulled his pistol from its holster.

"Calm down, I'm only carrying out the lieutenant's orders."

The barrel of the weapon successively threatened each one of those who continued to advance.

"Now you dare to attack women? What further villainies are you capable of?

"Don't get alarmed. The officer only wants to ask her a few questions about her brother."

Totally encircled, Onion-Head began to panic. His brandished pistol intimidated no one.

"Let go of that girl and go back to your master. You'll be a lot better off."

"Be reasonable. If you try to oppose the lieutenant's orders, you know you'll be sorry."

With a sudden twist, Ourida wrested her hand from his vise-like grip.

"I forbid you to put your dirty paws on me," she snapped scornfully at her guard.

Then, hurrying away from the turncoat, she told us, "I'm going to see that Roumi. He doesn't scare me one bit."

At that instant, Aïssa's wife vanished and then came running back with a veil for Ourida.

"Take this, cover yourself."

But the girl haughtily rejected the offer.

"That lieutenant does not belong to the community of the Prophet. That means he is not a man, and I do not have to hide my body from his view."

And, denuded, she strode along under the sun, more arrogant than its rays, more dazzling than its light.

We never learned the details of what happened at the French military annex. The apprehended men were interrogated for a long time, sometimes tortured; then they silently straggled back one after the other, to go about their daily business. None of them was willing to discuss what they had experienced after their arrests. But we were still waiting for Ourida to come back. After his release, Aïssa the cripple, who was worried about her, repeatedly asked to see the officer. He was not admitted. At each of his attempts, the sentinel guarding the entrance to the villa drove him away brutally. Aïssa was not even allowed to see his adopted daughter.

Two months later, Georgeaud was summoned to the French military headquarters. Onion-Head had accused him of supplying food and shoes to the underground people. Although skeptical, the lieutenant had nevertheless insisted on hearing the grocer out. Georgeaud told him, "You must know that I went to fight the Germans for your sake. I spent two years buried in the trenches, lying in wait for your enemies. When the armistice was signed at last, I was abandoned in a city and I didn't even know its name. In order to survive, I had to haul concrete that was heavier than our yearning for the happy valley. I lost my name, for Georgeaud is the surname of the man whose wheelbarrow I used. I also lost my memory, even though its roots alone supply the sap to nourish our exiled existence. My reminiscences of youth blurred, and the faces of my family and friends dissolved. I hoped to revive them, and so every evening I went and spent half my day's wages on a green beverage. Living there, I eventually got used to seeing no sun for the better part of the year, drinking no tea, walking in the rain, counting my money, eating fat pork, which makes your breath foul. I had even abjured my turban and strolled bareheaded despite the cold that made my ears freeze, my nose run, and my eyes tear. Then one day, when I had no job and no food, I was so sick of everything that I went and boarded the ship.

You have no idea. After more than twenty years, the sun and my childhood friends were waiting. They welcomed me as if I had just left the previous night. In the village, I quickly regained the serenity of living with one's own people. I did not participate in your last war against the Germans. Nonetheless, I learned that the most valorous of your fathers joined the underground to fight against the occupying forces. Our adolescents have merely followed their lead. I did not supply food and shoes to those men of the night. Because they did not ask me for anything. However, if they had asked me, I believe I would have done it."

Georgeaud was released one hour later. But when he reached the fig-tree square, his face was so livid that most of us drew ourselves up.

"What did they do to you?"

The grocer silently shook his head, then reached out to unhook the gugglet that was hanging from a low branch of the fig tree. After quaffing a generous bumper of water, he wiped his lips and sat down among us.

"They did nothing to me," he finally replied. "The lieutenant simply asked me a few questions."

"You look like a man who's just encountered Azraël."

Georgeaud took time for a deep breath.

"I saw Slimane's daughter," he said.

He told us that upon turning a bend in a corridor, he had run into Ourida; she was on her knees, holding a large rag and washing and rewashing a floor that large boots kept muddying up.

"She stared at me beseechingly for a long time," he went on, "before resuming her work. Was she entreating me to say nothing or, just the opposite, was she begging me to inform you of her torment? I lowered my head and left."

The next day, no one seemed to notice that Aïssa had vanished. Two days later, the cripple came hobbling back, more taciturn than usual, and entrenched himself with his press. None of us dared to interrogate him. Finally, after the dusk prayer, the imam decided to ask him the question.

"Were you able to see him? Is he still alive?" He slowly shook his head.

"The Beni Hadjar blocked my path. They prevented me from reaching the village."

"What happened then?"

"I was so insistent that they promised me they'd tell him."

"So the rumor is true? Old Hassam is still alive?"

During those tumultuous years, our nocturnal silence was so often disrupted by gunfire. But that night, we sensed that the detonations were closer than normal. When we came out in the morning (the imam had surreptitiously pushed back the time of the dawn prayer to make it coincide with the end of curfew), our puzzled and worried looks sought one another.

A bit later, the lieutenant visited the imam. He arrived on foot, alone, his face flaunting an unwonted friendliness.

"Onion-Head is dead," he announced to the sheik. "May we bury him in your cemetery?"

"That man betrayed his brethren but not his God. He has his place among the Muslims."

"Would you be willing to recite the prayer for the dead?"

"Allah alone can judge his acts, and forgive or punish."

Although satisfied, the officer remained sitting at the imam's side.

"I know there's a strange story circulating through the region about an immortal bandit. You're a man of faith and reason: do you lend any credence to that tale?"

"I believe in God and in his Apostle."

"Has any of you ever really encountered him?"

"Where? Since your arrival here, we have not been allowed to leave the village without authorization. You won't even let us harvest the olives in our most distant fields. So where could we possibly have encountered him?"

The officer requested and obtained a reinforcement of a dozen men. During the next few days, the squad searched the surrounding mountains with a fine-tooth comb. The village of the Beni Hadjar was under strict surveillance. Finally, the tribe of redheads was ordered to move to a regroupment camp near Sidi Bounemeur, and their hovels were instantly leveled.

The officer's relentlessness was futile. The man they were hunting remained elusive.

Actually, we did not learn what had happened that night until many years later, after the return of the little lawyer, who was extremely reluctant to describe those events.

After killing the sentinel, Hassan El Mabrouk entered the villa. He ran into Onion-Head, who was sleeping in the corridor. No sooner did the sergeant's eyes open than they turned up. His neck broken, he collapsed upon his mattress. Hassan El Mabrouk burst into the room of the little lawyer, who, awakening with a start, tried to get up. He was shoved back on his pillow by the palm of the giant, who left and dashed upstairs. Aiming his rifle, he crashed into the first room.

And Hassan El Mabrouk reemerged, lowering his rifle and his head, and melted into the night, assailed by gunfire from the stirred-up harkis.

If you understood my language you would have certainly asked me what Hassan El Mabrouk saw in the room. The little lawyer hesitated for a long time before satisfying our curiosity. He spoke in hints and innuendoes.

Yes, in the room where he had just switched on the light, the lieutenant, who was heading toward the door, encountered the rifle barrel. At that point, Ourida, stark naked, leaped from the bed and dashed over to shield his body; her hair was disheveled, her arms were outspread.

"I beg you," she shrieked, "spare him."

YES, THAT IS the sad tale of proud Ourida, the grand-daughter of Hassan El Mabrouk.

But at the time, we knew nothing. One day, the little lawyer announced that Ourida was dead. We did not ask him a single question. Blonde Ourida was buried next to her father, Slimane.

Time trudged by, then all at once it seemed to speed up. Wild rumors began to circulate. There was quite a hullaba-loo at the French military annex. Numerous harkis were deserting, but that didn't bother the lieutenant. Next, we saw the little lawyer heading toward us.

"Have you gotten permission to associate with us again?"

"No, I've here to say goodbye."

"Are you being exiled somewhere else?"

"No, I'm free."

"How come?"

"We've won."

"Won?"

"Yes, our country is independent. The French are leaving."

"The Roumis are beaten? Despite their intelligence, their matériel, and all the renegades they managed to rally to their cause? What did the men of the night oppose them with? How did they do it?"

"You were the ones who told me the story of the mountebank. Do you remember what he said: Victory often belongs to the more resolute and not the more powerful."

"That old Jew managed to discredit his own words. So
he was right after all? We would never have dreamed it
could be possible in our lifetime. The Roumis seemed rooted
here for centuries, and the passing of time merely consolidated their presence. So they're leaving after all?"

"They're leaving."

"We won't have to pay taxes anymore."

"You won't have to suffer injustice anymore."

"And who's going to run the country now?"

"Men who are chosen by the people."

"People like him and me, like Djelloul the blacksmith,
Aïssa the cripple, or Georgeaud back from exile? Are they
capable of choosing? It's really unsettling."

A few weeks later, we saw some of the people who had
stolen away from us and melted into the night: now they
were armed and uniformed, and they had attained a matu-
rity that sparked our admiration.

"Where are the others?" we asked them.

"Dead or vanished. They're martyrs."

I believe there was a shameful sense of relief at the news
that Omar El Mabrouk was gone.

"The Roumis are beaten," they told us. "They're all
returning to the country they came from. And we are finally
going to rediscover the valley of rosemary and singing well-
springs. Prepare to depart."

But the wisest among us explained to them that we no
longer wished to leave this denuded place which had welcomed us and enabled us to survive; that we had ultimately
grown attached to our rocky slopes, our emaciated olive
trees, our tutelary eucalyptuses; that we had learned to live
in deprivation and drudgery; and that we feared our virtues

would melt in contact with ease and abundance.

"Let those who want to leave leave, we will accompany them with our best wishes. We will give them all the documents attesting to our legal ownership of the lands in the valley of horehound and succulent grass. We will gladly turn our rights over to them."

They managed to convince several families to join them. They piled their belongings into the carts abandoned by the colonists, and, when the moment arrived, they came to us.

"Soon," they affirmed, "you will join us. Now that we have recovered our sovereignty, no one can contest our ownership of the valley of oregano and tender evenings. Once we're settled, we'll send for you. And our tribe will be reunited in the bosom of the happy valley."

It was a joyful return. All the villages they traveled through were celebrating. They were welcomed with open arms. En route, they encountered other migrants who, like them, were journeying to other valleys. At each resting place, they would gather round a huge bonfire and take pleasure in blending their dreams until late at night.

And then, one clear morning, they discovered at their feet the soft curves of the valley of ancestors and nostalgia. But, to their amazement, the valley offered nothing but the rectilinear stripes of fields of vineyards.

"Where are the seas of wheat, the almond orchards, the rose laurel hedges, the elegant firs, the immense and rebellious ash trees, the generous pomegranate trees, the wooded mantles of hills teeming with hares and boars? What has become of them? Could our fathers have lied to us?"

On all sides, they could make out nothing but a dreary alignment of vinestocks.

The springs had run dry, the wells had been filled in, the brooks no longer carried anything but the red refuse of wine cellars and distilleries.

"Not even the grass is growing now. What have they done to our valley?"

They didn't know that since a wicked law had prohibited the irrigation of vineyards, the colonists had left springs and wells in utter neglect. They didn't know that the knotty vinestock endured no grass and no shadow around it, that wherever it took root, the trees would fall and the grassland retreat.

The most ardent did not hold back.

"Who cares! We're not afraid of hard work. We'll tear out those sacrilegious plants with our own hands and sow barley and wheat and plant jasmine and almond trees."

They set to work. But on the third day, gendarmes came and hauled them off to a court of law.

"You are charged with destruction of public property. You will have to pay a fine for each vinestock you have torn out."

"But these are *our* lands!"

They produced the deeds. The judge laughed in their faces.

"Your old parchments are illegible."

"They've come down to us from our fathers' fathers."

"They don't give you any rights. Every proprietary deed must, under pain of being declared void, be duly notarized and registered with the county clerk. These lands to which you lay claim have been sequestered, transferred, or sold, and then repeatedly purchased and repurchased. Today, having been abandoned by their last owner, they have legally become government property."

"But these properties were stolen because our tribe rose up against the invader. It's perfectly natural for us to recover our patrimony."

"I understand," the judge responded, "but your request is judicially inadmissible."

As a special favor, they were offered jobs as farmhands in the nationalized farms. But they replied that they had no desire and no knack for getting tortured vinestocks to produce heavy clusters, for transforming the pulpy berries into those red or white liquors that make you lose your mind and your sense of restraint. They added that as far back as they could remember, none of them had ever accepted this new mercenary system, they all preferred even the disappointing results of voluntary effort to the security of a salary with alienating conditions.

They debated on and on about what they should do.

"We can't go back to Zitouna. We'd be disgraced."

"But whom can we turn to? The judges today resemble the colonial ones and they use the same language."

They agreed to send a delegation to the capital and explain the matter to the little lawyer.

"The city is immense. Where will we find him?"

"Supposedly, he's become an important person. The inhabitants must all know him."

The policeman guarding the entrance to the building didn't know what to make of these unkempt and ragged men who talked in an incomprehensible patois. He foisted them on the janitor. The latter spoke their language.

"I come from the countryside too," he announced amiably. "What can we do for you?"

"We want to see the little lawyer."

"Do you have an appointment?"

The envoys shrugged.

The janitor absented himself for some ten minutes and then returned with a secretary, to whom he handed them over. She concealed them in a room, where they remained, exercising their patience, sitting well-behaved on their chairs, wordless, motionless, until the moment the door opened.

"What are you doing here?" the newcomer asked them.

They explained the reason for their presence.

"How long have you been here?"

"Since this morning."

"But it's night now, and there's no one here. The offices are closed. I'm the watchman."

He paused to scratch his head.

"I'm obliged to see you out."

"Where should we go?"

Their interlocutor kept maltreating his scalp, and his eyes grew more and more pitying.

"The minister has gone home. He lives a stone's throw from here. I can show you the building so long as you never let on that I told you."

A little boy opened the door. The former exile promptly arrived and instinctively placed his hand on the child's shoulder in a protective and parental gesture.

"Yes?"

He didn't remember them. The four men reminded him that they had been the most attentive to his speeches at the saint's mausoleum in Zitouna. He apologized profusely upon hearing about their day of misadventures.

"All these people around us are supposed to help us. But actually, we're their hostages. They're the ones who decide whom we can or cannot see. According to them, our schedules are jammed up and we have major problems to solve. The truth of it is that I'm often bored for hours on end in my office, while downstairs my assistants fend off people who want to talk to me. Not to mention the fact that no one has any chance of crossing the threshold of my apartment house without a suit and tie. They've too quickly forgotten the maquis from which we come."

The puny lawyer looked ridiculous amid the stately furnishings of the immense room. He remained shivering and shriveled in his overcoat despite the very mild temperature.

"The dampness in this city is bad for me. It awakens all the old aches I developed in dark cells with sweating walls. These responsibilities that force me to keep crazy hours are no help in improving my condition. I think I'm going to return to your village and live there."

After hearing them out, the manikin became pensive. Finally he told them, "You can't expect this country to turn back the calendar one and a half centuries. It's illusory to believe that we can wipe away the past."

"You're talking like the judge who just passed judgment on us."

"It's the voice of reason. The happy valley never existed. It's a creation of your nostalgia for the past. You have to look toward the future and return to Zitouna, where you were all born. That's where you have to set about building and starting all over again, not in the valley from which you were driven."

However, refusing to endure the shame of returning empty-handed, they left the valley of grapes and evil-smelling cellars and scattered in the city.

During the next few years, the son of Ali, now mailman and sole reader of the newspaper, repeatedly showed us the photo of the frail lawyer.

"He has definitely become a cold-dweller."

And then one day, the little lawyer showed up here again, flanked by two policemen and holding the same suitcase. He was lodged in the same room at the same villa.

He had gotten even skinner and tinier. His gestures had grown even more uncertain. But, in that wrecked body, his eyes remained as incandescent as ever.

"Are you really this sick?" we asked him.

He nodded for a long time as we gaped incredulously.

"Yes, very sick," he replied. "My body has again experienced the same prison cells which are as damp as ever. But I still believe that attacks on freedom and denials of justice are to be condemned no matter where they come from."

We had no idea what he meant, but we welcomed him warmly. He went back to studying our old manuscripts and other even more secret books that were sent to him from abroad, and that the frowning policemen leafed through before reluctantly handing them to him. Soon he was more intimately conversant with the ancient history of our tribe than our best memorialists, which was bound to ignite a few disputes. Since our mnemotechnicians were the only people able to find their bearings in the inextricable tangle of family affiliations, their memories made them highly important in the devolutions of inheritances. However, the annals touted by the lawyer would sometimes raise serious questions. The most reasonable among us made it clear to him that the merciless irrecusability of the written word packed less clout for us than untrustworthy and generous memory, which managed to correct the most flagrant injustices.

"We certainly have our suspicions about these errors. But what good is truth if it adds to injustice? Our customs permit us to temper the rigors of the law with equity, which avoids condemning a man to poverty while his brother lives in opulence."

He went along with us, abandoning the old manuscripts to their dust, and proceeded to study foreign languages.

"You already know our language and that of the Koran, just as you speak and write that of the Roumis. Isn't that enough for you?" we asked him.

Since he had never challenged the imam's opinions, it took us a long time to discover the imam's veiled enmity toward him.

"That man is highly skilled in everything. But he does not believe in God."

The shivering exile believed, more than anything, in an ensemble of subtle and complex rules transcribed in a document that was supposedly known to all, and whose strict enforcement he relentlessly advocated. His return to our village resulted from his obstinacy in defending the weak, the penniless, the outlawed, the miserable. He unhesitatingly offered to represent the lepers in a riproaring lawsuit against the government. But we talked him out of it, knowing that such an affair could only get him exiled to an even more desolate place.

That was the reason we were beside ourselves to learn that on the occasion of an august visit, these men, who were flustered by their own importance, demanded the removal of our guest.

"Are those people too that scared of you? We thought you were one of them."

"They're scared of everything: from their wives and their shadows and their most unconditional supporters to their enemies. But what they're most scared of is the voice of justice."

At the arrival of the policemen who were assigned to escort him, we silently massed in front of the villa. Our threatening glares and Omar El Mabrouk's desire to avoid any incident prompted them to negotiate. They finally agreed that it was enough for the lawyer to promise not to go out that day.

On the appointed morning, civil and military vehicles, trucks, tanks, and a swarm of helicopters began pouring into our village, not to mention soldiers and policemen, photographers and journalists, and other, even more important men, who gave the impression of knowing the exact age of a camel colt.

When the throng advanced toward the small stele, we noted that Omar El Mabrouk was way back in the last row, jostled by the crowd, yet affable and beaming, obsequious and servile, helpful and timorous.

"You just don't realize," he subsequently told Mohamed, "how many rungs there are on the power ladder. You can climb all the way up to the sky, and there'll still be people above you."

THE NEXT DAY, the foreigners got to work with their herculean engines. From the enormous quantities of fruits and vegetables they purchased, we inferred that they must be drawing incredible salaries. But they did not appreciate the flesh of our sheep or goats. They preferred to send away for their own meat in huge frozen quarters.

"It's because they come from the lands of snow," the blacksmith concluded with his customary sagacity. "During the shorter part of the year, their streams and fountains are frozen and stop singing. That's why the foreigners are so sad."

They asked to recruit a few workers among us. During an inspection visit, Omar El Mabrouk took it upon himself to explain the details of our labor laws.

"You have to be fair and employ one man per family. They're willing to accept the minimum wage, but don't be surprised at their nonchalance: they have never considered work an end in itself. You will give them breaks for their daily prayers and their annual vacation during the olive-picking season."

Needless to say, we refused to cooperate. The salaries they offered did tempt a few lepers. But the terrifying engines dissuaded them from approaching.

Within a few weeks, our familiar landscape was turned topsy-turvy: hills flattened, ravines filled in, rocks pulverized, forests razed, roads straightened. The foreigners proved indefatigable.

"Don't they ever rest? And why are they so relentless?"

We protested vociferously when they planned to level our cemetery. The foreign megaphone declared, "Stop worrying, we only want to move it to a less intrusive place. We respect your beliefs and your rites. On the basis of the meticulous studies that were effectuated, we can guarantee that the bones of your ancestors will recover their exact original positions, so their shades can rest in peace. As a bonus, we will place a lovely marble slab on every single grave. In any case, you are powerless to oppose us. We have bought all your weapons and all your saddles."

"We didn't know the value of those heirlooms," the master of the forge commented bitterly.

The foreigners even threatened to use their electric saw on our tutelary eucalyptuses. The lawyer, who had learned their language from books, was willing to plead our case with them. It was a waste of effort.

"They're not interested and they're very pressed for time. They're afraid they'll have to pay the huge late fees stipulated in the contract."

Our indignant women stirred up the flames of our revolt, and each adult male was tied to a tree trunk, with the exception of the imam. We were untied only for prayers and meals: our religious leader had left his mosque and our housewives their homes to come and comfort our spirits and bodies. Each man ate or communed by his tree. The concert of birds supported our cause, but their droppings soiled our turbans. The foreigners' megaphone advised, pleaded, threatened. But it was useless. Their representative went to Sidi Bounemeur to telegraph the cold-dwellers, reminding them that they had been assured of the total amenableness of the indigenous populace and threatening to invoke the terrifying clauses in the secret rider of the contract.

The next day, Omar El Mabrouk made a foray into our village. He was more furious than a wounded boar.

"What's going on here?" he yelled as he climbed out of his car.

The most courageous among us explained to him:

"These eucalyptuses were planted by our forebears during the first few days when they settled in this desolate place. The trees grew quickly while everything around them wilted. Thus, they gratified the exiles with hopes of shade and survival. The quick growth of these little trees probably gave our vanquished ancestors the strength to confront adversity. Today, these trees make the wind and the birds sing, they are an indulgent refuge for our moments of rest, and they provide antiseptic leaves for the baths of the lepers. These trees cannot be touched."

The perfect's booming laugh frightened the birds out of their insouciance, and they hastily fluttered away. He slowly advanced toward us, his chest puffed up, his hands on his hips.

"I didn't realize you were this courageous. Where were you, oh my brave heroes, when my father was groaning in the clutches of the bear? Did anyone see you, oh my daredevils, take up arms against the colonizer and face his regiments more numerous than the cells of a beehive, his stubbornly charging armored vehicles, his planes more furious than a startled wasp? No, you preferred to keep your rifles and combat equipment in a warm place in order to sell them to people who'll treat them as museum exhibits."

He took off his glasses.

"You sons of whores! I'll screw every last one of you in broad daylight and then go on to your virgins and your wives. You're going to learn that as of now there is one person of authority in this place and only one: me. And before you so much as fart or wipe your snot, you're going to have to ask my permission."

Then he suddenly appeared to mellow.

"Be reasonable. You know very well that these birds loot your barley fields and olive trees, and their cheeping disturbs your siestas. Your own mayor reached an agreement with me. Not to mention that leprosy contaminated all the trees after you heedlessly permitted the outlaws to settle in the forest. Just look at those leaves. They're being nibbled by a dry mold, which has made them lose their natural silveriness. At the least caprice of the wind, the fine particles scatter through the atmosphere. For some time now, you've been breathing them in without realizing it. You've probably caught the disease. I wonder if it's not already too late. Those eucalyptuses have to be chopped down as fast as possible."

He strolled among us for an instant and burst into guffaws upon recognizing the son of Messaoud.

"You too among them? I thought you were cowardly enough to always find a pretext for skedaddling. Is it your new position that's made you so bold?"

The prefect began untying him.

"You are mayor of this town," he murmured sweetly, "and my representative. Your role is to make sure the populace doesn't get on the wrong tack like this. You've failed. And so you're fired."

He tossed the rope over the ex-mayor's shoulder.

"In consideration of your position, I allowed you to live in the villa which you and the imam were inhabiting without permission. You are now going to return to your ancestral shack after paying up all the back rent. Your lecherous offspring will no longer be spending his nights pounding his fiancée in back of the wash-house. From now on, I'm going to take personal charge of the administration of Zitouna. In this connection, I've noticed the unsanitary conditions in your tavern. It does not meet the legal hygiene standards."

"What do you mean?"

"It does not have running water in accordance with regulations."

"Running water?"

"It does not have the obligatory water closet."

"But we always take care of our needs out in nature. We don't even have what they call accommodations in our homes."

"The law must be respected everywhere. Your premises are hereby closed for a period of three months. Your reopening will be contingent on your adding the necessary facilities."

And Omar El Mabrouk headed back to his car. After replacing his glasses on his nose, he turned around and told us:

"As for you poor shits, you can stay where you are. The saws are coming. They'll cut through every trunk, human or vegetable."

The forest was razed. The birds that lived there emigrated en masse. Henceforth, we awoke at every dawn to the silence of a global catastrophe. All we had now was the promise of three fig trees to tempt our daily rest. The lepers declared themselves healed and went to work en masse for the foreigners. Receiving their salaries regularly, they learned how to snub us.

Day after day, the foreign engines altered our countryside. When they planned to blow up our olive trees, Omar El Mabrouk came to see us.

"There's no reason to take it so tragically. These grasping shrubs rewarded your drudgery with sickly fruits. Besides, now that the cripple's oil mill is shut down, I don't see what you can do with your crops. In any case, you'll be generously indemnified. The government agents will soon come and assess the value of every acre and every tree. You'll get a gold mine, and it'll allow you to make the fondest of your old wishes come true: you can visit the Holy Places, perhaps with the signal favor of passing away there, or you can put on a sumptuous wedding for your youngest adolescent with the virgin he desires."

"But what can we live on?"

"Don't worry. I've thought it out. I promise you that in this countryside at the end of the world, I will send for machines that will pierce the clay and the shale and penetrate to the very bottom to look for water and make it spurt forth in its primary force. You can then grow sweet licorice, fragrant cantaloupes, hot pepper, fragile beans, demanding tomatoes, pears that are juicier than the lips of your first beloved. You will become rich and fat."

The harvest was several days off, but Omar El Mabrouk's policemen refused to allow us into the fields.

"I know very well that you were secretly conniving with Aïssa to bring him your olives so he can work his mill at night."

Deprived of their favorite food, the starlings migrated in their turn, to the great sorrow of the blacksmith's youngest son, a past master with the slingshot: with unequaled precision, his stones decimated the swarms of olive lovers. By protecting our crops, he amassed necklaces of game, which he peddled to the drivers motoring along the highway. The useful scamp thus had to put away his catapult, but he still refused to join his father at the forge.

Some time later, the cripple died, his heart broken by inactivity. When the four men heaved up his coffin, we realized that none of us knew the road to the new cemetery. All our paths had been modified, embanked, straightened, or eliminated. In their misleading promise, new, rectilinear roads offered themselves to our confusion. We scattered through the countryside, each of us guided by his instinct.

This brought home to us how thoroughly our universe had been perverted.

There was nothing left to go by. The roads had changed their routes, the mountains their locations. The plains had buckled, the hills flattened. The south had altered its position, the sky its color, the sun its passage, time its speed. The climate had inverted its seasons.

After finally reaching the cemetery, the coffin-bearers, followed by several helpers, waited endlessly for the arrival of the imam, the only man who knew how to recite the prayer for the dead. But he never showed up. At twilight, they decided to bury the oil presser without the customary incantations.

By the time we got back to the village, it was nightfall: we were haggard, bewildered, incapable of finding our bearings.

It finally struck us that Omar El Mabrouk was right. The fine dust of the eucalyptuses had affected our minds. Upon returning, we found that words had changed meaning, children their sex, adults their age, women their husbands, men their trades and fortunes.

That, I believe, was the day on which we started becoming aware of the ravages caused by the arrival of Omar El Mabrouk.

AS SOON AS their work was done, the foreigners loaded up their materials and vanished as suddenly as they had come. They did not even have the good manners to say goodbye to us.

The most sagacious among us stated, "They will never understand us. They live by the dictates of bookkeeping and they are always astonished at the generosity on which our life is based. Now that they've pocketed their checks, they've lost all interest in us. We won't see them again until the signing of the next contract. They could at least have returned our rifles and saddles."

Drawn by the villas that had been put up, the civilized men began reappearing. In time, we got to know them very well. They seemed intent on thoroughly resembling foreigners who have just left home. They went bareheaded despite the cruel rays of the sun, their long hair played in the wind, indecently hiding their foreheads and tickling their eyes. They pretended to be comfortable in tight suits that hemmed in not only their torsoes but also their thighs, and they were unaware of the impropriety of those tapered trousers which sculpted the bulges of their genitals. They failed to greet passersby, they went their way with hangdog looks as if preoccupied with terrible anxieties. Subsequently, we learned that for them a member of the community of the

Prophet was less real than those ink creatures that stuck to paper and that they valued so unreasonably. Thus, despite the most elementary rule of civilized behavior, they could remain with their heads buried in their documents when a visitor entered their offices. They could waste hours arguing over pure abstractions instead of devoting themselves to the commentaries on the words and deeds of the Lawgiver. For them, nothing existed until it was translated into signs. They ignored the most blatant fact, the most irrefutable verity, the most unimpeachable evidence, and they put their trust in unfathomable and laughable scribblings. They were loath to express themselves in the tongue of the Tiding. It was only much later that we realized they did not speak it. Needless to say, they did not grasp a word of our language. This explained why whenever one of us, knowing he was in the wrong, was called on the carpet, he would use only his mother tongue. Exasperated, the civilized men would dismiss him. As for them, they preferred using the jargon of the Roumis even when talking to their wives and children.

We recognized that these were people without faith. You never saw them at the mosque, not even for Friday prayers, not even for the prayers of Aïd, much less for rain prayers. We subsequently learned not only that many of them consumed forbidden beverages, but that they actually brought the bottles home and sipped those beverages shamelessly and unconscionably, in full sight of their spouses and offspring.

The civilized men had no honor. They let their wives go out alone and denuded, with no protection or surveillance whatsoever. These women went to the village grocery on their own and, without veiling their faces or lowering their eyes, ordered the products they desired from Georgeaud. However, it was often a wild-goose chase, for the veteran's shelves still offered only a meager selection. So they would take their abulic husband's car and drive off to Sidi Bounemeur.

With more and more of the civilized people settling here, Georgeaud rapidly adjusted to the new demand, which was so much more lucrative. He stocked up on those gaudy packages that obstinately camouflaged their contents, providing a cold and impalpable image, and thus inaugurating the era of generalized swindling, which made people prefer shadow to substance. Georgeaud began to slight, then scorn his traditional clientele, which limited itself to buying sugar, coffee, salt, and a few grams of spices. Whenever a civilized woman walked in, the grocer would wink coarsely at us, as if inviting us to an unparalleled spectacle while simultaneously forewarning us of its parodistic nature. He thereby incited our complicity, using it as a pretext to wait on her first. A sudden joviality transfigured his face, and, using the language of the Roumis, he ostentatiously greeted the newcomer, while we modestly lowered our heads. Next, he began vaunting the new products that he had just gotten in and whose prices he had hiked indecently.

"Why do we have to treat them with kid gloves? They earn more in a month than we do in a year. They don't give a damn about the prices of items, they buy them like mistakes in addition."

We had not learned duplicity. Despite his age, Georgeaud was merely going down in our esteem. We were not taken in by his play-acting. We preferred the man who had received us in his shop without feeling obligated to smile at us or push us to buy, and who, lying under the fig trees, let us serve ourselves, just as he was the first to rant and rail against the suppliers when he was forced to raise the price of an article.

Thus, it was not long before he knocked down the wall

separating his shop from that of the burnoose-embroiderer,
whose eyesight was dimming, and who, in the course of
time, had lost his clientele and was now living on our disguised charity. The moment his business had petered out,
several of us had chipped in to prevent the old man from
ending his days in penury. Georgeaud's arrogance grew as
big as his turnover, and we discovered how thoroughly his
foreign exile had perverted his soul.

We are modest, but tolerant. Our oldest men could not
help being offended by the getup of the wives of the civilized
men: these women left their arms bare up to their armpits
and their legs down to their knees, and, for love of provoca-
tion or perversion, seemed to favor blouses that made their
breasts stand out and skirts that hugged their buttocks so
tightly that the passerby knew all there was to know about
their anatomies and could undress them with his eyes.

But we understood that their wardrobe and behavior
were due to an unfortunate mimicry. Forgetful of the Messenger's teachings, the civilized men lived with their eyes
glued on foreign cities, where many of them had been edu-
cated and spent their adolescence. With an ineffable nostalgia for their juvenile emotions, they yearned for those lands
of tenderness and amorous strolls along the embankments of
big rivers. They thus associated their loveliest memories of
youth with those countries. In the lecture halls of universities, their professors had incited them to give up our virtues
in favor of the values of science, efficiency, and output.
Along the streets, the arms of beautiful girls snuggling
against them covered the austere displays with desire.

Everything begins with the woman—we have known
that for a long time.

But it never struck them that their new values, drawn
from foreign knowledge, would artfully sap the roots of
their being. They thus condemned themselves to living in

disarray and fragmentation, incapable of distinguishing between that which constituted their essence and that which had molded them. They forgot where they came from, and they had no idea where they were going.

They had lost their souls. God will pity those who have gone astray.

We have retained the Apostle's teachings about women. We know they have no piety. Their minds are more frequently impure than their vaginas. Wrapped up in the things of this world, they live commonplace lives, unconcerned about the day of Resurrection. Our Prophet and wisdom insist on keeping them within their natural roles: procreation and housekeeping. While they have the job of raising our children, they do not educate them. We make sure to remove our little males from their mothers' apron strings as soon as possible; indeed, from their very first steps, we urge all our boys to go outdoors and practice the games of virility together.

Although we insist that our wives and daughters respect our religious rituals, we have never tried to impose our faith on them. We don't quite know what the image of a prostrate woman might suggest.

Our ancestors warned us: A beautiful girl is a calamity. We concluded that a respectable maiden has to conceal her charms until her wedding day and then henceforth reserve them for her spouse. Being aware of the dangers of passion, we advise our young husbands to take their wives at night, in darkness, to avoid indulging in those perverse games that derange and enslave. We keep close watch on the behavior of our newlywed adolescents, and if we often tease them about their unwonted eagerness to hurry home, our goal is not to ridicule them. We are simply intent on making them realize that masculine dignity enjoins a man to hide from others, and especially from his wife, the feelings she inspires.

By controlling himself and by controlling her, he will benefit from the esteem of others and from her admiration.
Alone, but especially in company, he must know how to
ignore her, bawl her out, and, if necessary, humiliate her. A
man who succumbs to his wife's charms is doomed. We have
known such husbands galore—the valiant turned cowardly,
the generous turned covetous, the wise turned insane, the
miserly prodigal, the prudent reckless, and so many more.

Women are diabolical.

A respectable wife does not have to use tricks to excite
her master's love. She must remain natural, not adorn herself
with jewels, she must reject all those products that mask the
faults of the face, illuminate the cheeks, enlarge the eyes, or
brighten the color of the lips.

The civilized women were experts in the art of self-
transformation. The lepers' wives who worked in those
homes were flabbergasted by the metamorphoses of those
women. They would see them get out of bed with disheveled hair, wan faces, narrow eyes, curdled cheeks, thick lips.
One hour later, the leper's wife would discover a vivacious
and ravishing woman, who would shower her with orders
before slamming the door.

The civilized women hated staying at home. They
wanted to get out and see the world. They loved staying up
late. Some of them, emulating their husbands, would work
outside the house from dawn to dusk, neglecting their
homes and children for a salary, even though their husbands
earned a splendid living. But there was something even
worse. Many of those women refused to procreate, they
would take permissiveness pills which canceled the effects of
the act, and no husband dared to repudiate them.

Left to their own devices, their few offspring became
brats. They were brazen, fearing no adults and insolently
talking back whenever they were reprimanded. Their fa-

thers not only spoiled them rotten, but blew up if anyone dared to correct their children.

We have none of those problems. We insist on the respect that is owed to our elders, and any man whatsoever could thrash a child right in front of his father, who would neither be upset nor take exception to it.

In the early days, those delicate tots, deserting their squeaky clean villas, would venture toward our hovels. They felt thrills of delight upon discovering our strange lifestyle. Our own kids, initially cautious, were not long in approaching them. Language difficulties were easily overcome, and solid friendships developed, for the new friends often arrived clutching a snack that they didn't care to finish or with pockets full of goodies that didn't seem to tempt them. The village children were astonished at how readily those boys parted with their provisions. They gave them away nonchalantly, sometimes they seemed relieved; while our children would suffer the worst violence rather than let go of their piece of biscuit or handful of figs. Those who pushed and shoved to take their place at the common bowl of couscous didn't realize that their comrades were scolded and punished if they didn't lick their plates clean. Our children knew how to exploit those tots. But the friendships soon degenerated. Their games frequently turned into brawls, and the civilized kids would go home with torn cheeks, bloody noses, black eyes, and arms covered with bruises. Their mothers now ordered them not to play with the aborigines. Which induced our offspring to poke holes in the fence and visit them. Several young lepers were then recruited as guards and provided with uniforms similar in every respect to that of our constable. This terminated the period of abundant food for our village children.

After settling in, most of the civilized people wanted to take on our wives or daughters as their maids. We subtly explained that we could not have our women transformed into paid servants. They thought they could change our minds by offering higher wages.

A few of us expounded, "Despite their condition, we are intent on preserving the dignity of our females. We fully realize that they cannot resist gratuitous wickedness and material temptations. We may at times have to give them a good dressing-down, but they nevertheless constitute our gushing springs and the softest part of our livers. We refuse to see them kneeling at your feet, washing your floors."

However, during the next few days, we were dumbfounded to see that so many lepers had accepted the offers of the civilized people and agreed to hire out their wives and daughters.

This brought us a lot of trouble.

We lived poorly, but honorably. Now, the servant lepers, exploiting the credulity of their mistresses, never stopped complaining and lamenting. They started by begging for stale bread in order, they said, to feed their numerous siblings or children, as if they were starving to death; but actually, they used it to stuff their chickens in order to fatten them more quickly. Next they inherited the couple's old clothes, which they sold at a profit. And also their scrapped gadgets.

The civilized people soon came to regard us as greedy and stingy. Which merely reinforced their disdain for us. One day, when a civilized woman discovered that one of her small gold chains had vanished, she instantly suspected the girl who was working for her. She filed charges with the police in Sidi Bounemeur, who showed up, determined to search the home of the girl's parents from top to bottom.

Outraged, we advanced toward them. The most imposing member of our group explained to them that we had never known a theft or a thief in the memory of our tribe.

"A complaint has been brought," the police replied, "we have to investigate."

"If that woman maintains that some object has been filched from her home, then all of us here are prepared to indemnify her collectively."

"That's inadmissible. We have to proceed with our search."

Our imam personally vouched for the honorable character of the accused family.

However, the stubborn policemen merely did as they liked. They discovered the gold chain at the bottom of a pot.

"STOP ACTING like assholes. You'll wake my crab lice. Which you'll live to regret. And look around you. Even the biggest jerks would have to admit that there can't be any other seat for our prefecture."

Our imam, whom we had never thought of as so courageous, walked toward Omar El Mabrouk.

"This place contains the grave of our founding saint, who has kept watch over us for more than a century. He has always protected us."

"Protected you? From what, you poor fools? You've suffered hailstorms and epidemics, droughts and locusts, war and its anguish, famine and exile."

"But we have always survived."

Omar El Mabrouk's laughter would have terrified the birds that once resided in our eucalyptuses.

"That's a pack of superstitions. You're still living in the antiquated time of the valley of scillas and swallows. Yet you know that today your valley is nothing but vineyards and cellars with unbearable miasmas."

"Before his death, our saint recommended that we never build within one hundred yards of the olive tree."

"From now on, I will be the only saint you worship. And you can trust me: you won't lose in the exchange. I will lead you out of your darkness and into the light."

Omar El Mabrouk raised himself to his full height.

"You're a pain in the ass with your obsolete beliefs when I'm trying to make you happy, killing myself daily, from dawn to dusk, every minute of the day, working so hard that I have no time to see my children or visit my wives."

He went on, "Here, on this site, I'm going to build a school with tables and a rostrum, pictures on the walls and big windows facing the world. You will have no choice: you will have to bring your children here, each wearing a pinafore and carrying a satchel. With your own hands, you will push them toward the road of abjuration, and by the end of that road they will have forgotten their ancestors and become our allies. They will learn the language of the Roumis and mathematics, so they can count without the help of their fingers. They will be able to locate the most famous cities on a map of the world. They will be able to list the names of the different kinds of clouds and they will deduce that rain is not caused by prayers or incantations. They will practice music and singing, which are so heretical for you, and they will study a thousand other things whose existence you don't even suspect. Just like the city people, they will celebrate their birthdays, dance with girls, wangle their high school diplomas, and smoke little joints. Next door to the school there will be a supermarket with shelves offering a profusion of goods. You will taste bananas from the country of the Zandj; your babies will drink milk that has been miraculously changed into powder and that will turn to liquid again when mixed with water; your virgins will be tempted by beauty products; your children will be spellbound by toys; your women will obtain washing machines; and you will pay stiff prices for those apparatuses that make you laugh and cry and that will replace your storytellers little by little. A bit further on, we will build the new post office, with the son of Ali as postmaster, and, if you desire it, he will let you hear the voices of your sons exiled across the sea. Opposite the post office, a hospital will receive your pregnant women, vaccinate your newborn against all past and future illnesses, supply your newlyweds with free pills that make them sterile. Those of you with stomach ailments will go there to treat the ravages caused by their sorrowful moods; those who suffer from the sugar disease will no longer have to gorge themselves on bitter almonds. You will be given countless injections that alleviate pain, make the elderly frisky, let you sleep all day or stay up all night, or vice versa, whatever you wish. Coupled with that establishment, there will be a court of law, whose judge, instructed by written texts about all the things in the world, will settle all your conflicts equitably no matter how complex they may be, and he will know how to replace your disbanded djemaa advantageously. Well, tell me, what do you think?"

We knew that Georgeaud and the son of Ali agreed with Omar El Mabrouk, as did Mohamed, who still had hopes of regaining his position of mayor. We had learned to distrust the lepers. Although shocked, we were not surprised by their adherence. But we were dumbfounded to discover that a few of our sons were lured by the prefect's plans.

"By my special fiat, all the lepers who work on construction sites will be declared cured."

At a nod from Omar El Mabrouk, the bulldozers began to roar, spurting jets of black smoke, then slowly lumbered forward. The terrified imam recoiled and hurried off, scattering a volley of imprecations.

"You are cursed, you son of the devil!"

The echoes of Omar El Mabrouk's laughter punctuated the imam's retreat.

The prefect walked over to Mohamed and amiably took his arm.

"I am pleased to see," he told him, "that you are coming to your senses. With a bit of zeal and perseverance, you could regain your position and reopen your café. You were able to see that my opponents always lose. Half the population is willing to follow me. I'm counting on you to win over the reluctant ones. Don't forget that I hold grudges for a long, long time. I've never forgotten that your intolerant imam always prohibited my father from entering the mosque."

Omar stepped back and faced us squarely.

"Don't worry," he said. "I'm also planning to build a real mosque, with twin minarets, Méziane and Améziane will climb to their tops and summon you in chorus to services. The mosque will have a series of bathrooms with running water, hot and cold. Thick woolen carpets will caress your bare feet. You will no longer have to put up with that toothless old man who drools and splutters on your venerable turbans. I'm going to recruit an imam trained at the finest universities, remunerated appropriately, and his quicksilver rhetoric will fascinate you more than the breasts of the daughter of Rabat."

Certain of his victory, Omar El Mabrouk concluded:

"Those of you who want to turn your backs on progress can go home to your hovels. Those of us who are here must get to work."

Numerous lepers forged ahead on the construction site, drawn by the promise of getting priority at the new apartment buildings.

"You have to understand us: we are still living in tents, in winter snow and summer dust, without even the shelter of the eucalyptuses."

We replied, "You have only yourselves to blame. Our houses are so simple that they can be built in two days. All the materials are available, and we offered to lend you a hand. But you preferred putting your trust in false promises. When you arrived, we already suspected that you were carriers of an illness that is far more serious than the one they said you were stricken with. Yet we believed in the healing virtues of brotherhood."

A few of our sons also turned up on the embanked fields, inveigled by the assurance of steady jobs.

"If the olive trees are gone, what are we going to do all day long? And how can we make sure of feeding our children?"

There were many accidents on the construction site. Several people died. The laborers deserted, but Omar El Mabrouk sent for a squad of policeman and forced the defectors to go back to work.

The transformer niche was decorated with small flags, and Omar El Mabrouk invited us to the lighting ceremony. He arrived, stepping lively, escorted by a mob of civilized people. He was in a good mood.

"I promised," he said, "to lead you out of the darkness and into the light."

And he pulled down the switch amid the applause of his companions. The domes of the lamps lit up.

In the surrounding luminosity, that superfluous glow triggered a few derisive grimaces among us.

"Is that all? And we thought the earth was suddenly going to shake, forcing us to walk upside down despite our proverbial reserve."

We were mistaken. Far more cunning, far more ravaging than the dry eucalyptus mildew that we had inhaled, the additional brightness would throw our daily lives topsy-turvy.

"Wait till nightfall," someone commented.

"What good is it?" the blacksmith asked. "We normally get home and into bed after the twilight prayer. Is this going to make it easier for the dogs to chase us?"

But, sacrificing ourselves to the innovation, we waited until evening and then pretended to marvel at those wan halos that unmasked the night and left all objects indecently exposed. We felt embarrassed, like someone involuntarily stumbling on an intimate scene. We didn't dare look at one another. The diluted colors of objects increased our discomfort, and we were very anxious to get home.

The unusual brightness disrupted the lives of the few birds that, deeply rooted here like us, balked at migrating despite the disappearance of their traditional perches. Unable to tell night from day, they kept warbling incessantly until they dropped from exhaustion. The blacksmith's youngest son took it upon himself to gather them up. We assumed he was profiting from the windfall by peddling them to drivers along the highway. However, we were deeply moved to learn that he was taking them cross-country to bury them discreetly. Then the adolescent pulled his slingshot back out and aimed at the lamps mounted on stilts. His infallible missiles blinded the lights one by one.

After assessing the damage, Omar El Mabrouk, followed by the constable, who now tagged after him everywhere, challenged the enlaced fig trees with his stature.

"It's like trying to pull swine out of their shit. I now see I was wrong to drudge away like that. In any case, you're nothing but a pack of rebels. You can keep wallowing in your mud, I wash my hands of it. Things will work out in spite of you."

Then, turning to Rabah, he said, "You're gonna throw that brat in the clink for destruction of public property."

"But we don't have a jail."

"Are you gonna play games with me too? A squad of cops will be showing up here pretty soon, and you can go back to ticketing the donkeys that trespass on public roads.

You oughta know that the first building that's gonna go up here is the police station. It'll have a huge cellar with a whole row of cells. In the meantime, the delinquent is gonna keep the little lawyer company. You're gonna have the job of guarding him."

That was that, we thought, but the havoc continued without our knowing it. Two-wire systems began sneaking along, gaining house after house.

The son of Mohamed had his father's moustache, but he also had a business instinct, and he profited from the percolator he received from the foreigners: Mohamed had abandoned his café after it had been shut down by order of the prefect, and now his son took it over, transforming it from top to bottom. He installed a fridge to sell cold drinks, which were previously unknown, and he put in a counter, enabling customers to consume while standing, which compelled them to hurry. He replaced the mats with tables and chairs. To do so, he confiscated the ones under the fig trees, forcing us to stretch out in the dust. We had to protest loudly to Mohamed to make his son put them back. But the young man refused to take care of them. They remained exposed to the dampness of the night, the dust of the winds, the games of the cats who came and sharpened their claws. Very soon, the chairs and tables were in shreds.

Upon reopening the café, the son of Mohamed defied us by allowing cards and dominoes, and our adolescents took to them with a vengeance, playing until the wee hours of the night. In order to hold on to customers torn between temptation and their old habit of turning in early, he placed upon a console an apparatus for making you laugh and cry.

The growing number of regulars here could no longer wake up in time for their morning prayer. Most of them worked on the construction site, and the tight schedules forced them to give up their religious practices.

Georgeaud finally installed the obligatory electric sign on his shop and purchased an apparatus for making the sugar snow that the children of the civilized people adore. After tasting it warily, our children likewise got used to it. Since they couldn't hope to get the money from us to buy those lick treats, they began rummaging through the pockets of our djellabas at night. Within a few months, Georgeaud had struck it rich, and he set about building a both vast and misshapen house of brick and concrete on the land of his ancestors. The nightmarish edifice began to plague our nights. A delegation of his closest neighbors tried making him listen to reason.

"Your house keeps rising and growing and it still isn't finished. You shouldn't build that high. Your balconies are hanging over our courtyards, and you'll be able to see what our girls and women are doing. The Prophet recommended that we should try to distinguish ourselves by fervor and not by fortune."

Georgeaud retorted:

"It's envy that's making you talk like this. When I was in exile, you forgot all about me. I became a shopkeeper, you despised me. Now that I'm rich, you're jealous. I'm going to add another story just to spite you. Furthermore, I'm informing you that I will no longer extend credit to any of you. You'll have to pay for all your purchases in good drachmas and deniers."

The complainants referred the matter to the djemaa, which, after debating it at length, designated two of its members to negotiate with the grocer. But he gave them the cold shoulder.

"The meetings of your kangaroo court are illegal, and its decisions are null and void. If I notify the prefect, he'll punish you for reconstituting a disbanded association."

Once his immense residence was finally completed,

Georgeaud, feeling solitary, decided to take a wife. We agreed that there was nothing wrong with his marrying some lonely widow who would sweeten his twilight years by relieving him of the banal, everyday tasks that the old man probably disliked more and more.

"He must be fed up with preparing his morning and evening meals, sweeping his house, mending and washing his clothes."

Tempted by the grocer's fortune, several candidates tried their luck. But that was not what Georgeaud was after. He wanted a virgin of less than twenty. We pointed out to him that he was long in the tooth and white on top.

"Allah knows that we kept urging and urging you to start a family ever since you returned from exile. Your constant refusals led us to believe that you had some kind of handicap. Time has passed, and today you should think only of ensuring your sojourn in the afterlife."

"Life is in God's hands, and no one else has the right to fix its length. As for your other concern, I can assure you I have never suffered from any ailment. Over in France, I fornicated more furiously than a rutting buck. I still feel I'm in the prime of life and capable of having offspring. My wife-to-be can be certain of living a life of ease."

Needless to say, none of us was willing to satisfy the senile grocer's vagary. However, he did find a greedy leper who offered him his virgin—for a stupendous compensation, no doubt. Scandalized by the news, we gathered round the imam.

"More than Omar El Mabrouk, more than the lepers, more than our renegade sons, that man will draw all the misfortunes of heaven and earth to this place."

Our sheik dug in his heels.

"I refuse to recite the Fatiha for this unnatural union."

Georgeaud shrugged.

"I don't need your blessing. I'll go to town hall and have a civil ceremony."

The wedding took place in defiance of the villagers. None of us attended. The story had a tragic ending. The young wife, raised in the outlying slums of the city, began to imitate the conduct of the civilized women. She dressed and painted her face like them and went outdoors denuded. She began to visit them, staying longer and longer. The lepers employed as guards at the housing development spread rumors that she was also meeting bachelors there. Little by little, those men had the audacity to visit her at her home. One day, upon returning unexpectedly, Georgeaud caught one of his wife's lovers in the act. The lover had no trouble strangling the old man. We refused to alert the commissioner who had just settled in. Several feet from the fig-tree square, we put in a new cemetery, and that was where the grocer was buried.

AS SOON AS his house was completed, Omar El Mabrouk took up residence in Zitouna.

"You know," he confided to his secretary, "I was wrong to despise this post. I feel just fine and dandy here. This place is so godforsaken that no cold-dweller is going to come and stick his nose in my affairs. In case any diehards try to find their way here, they're sure to get lost. I've ordered my agencies not to put up any signpost. I want peace. The civilized people that I've recruited know they have to be at my beck and call no matter how important their positions may be. I chose them on the basis of their high frustration level. They were dragging about in the streets of the capital, their pockets stuffed with diplomas and their hearts seething with resentment. Some of them were jobless and all of them were homeless. A few were knocking themselves out to forget their knowledge; they were trapped in offices ignored by everyone; the children of the others were stowed away in basements and never saw the light of day. I offered them air-conditioned villas and jobs that lived up to their ambitions. They have no desire to lose either their villas or their jobs. They'll keep their traps shut. I made a point of locating and hiring the most hate-filled lepers. They know how to harass the villagers with no encouragement from me. Naturally, I made a point of summoning all my old henchmen from the maquis. All of them showed up. Those total stooges are used to protecting my sleep and my escapades. I know I can put my mind at ease. No one will stop me from scratching my balls when I get out of bed, or pissing on the rosebush that embellishes the stairs outside my residence, or farting in my sleep, or aiming the snot that clogs up my nostrils and spurting it over three feet away. I'm going to be a sex maniac again and send for all the Messalinas in the capital who gave me hard-ons but rejected my advances for fear of compromising themselves. They will be ecstatic. Far from the promiscuity of the city, here, among the peasants, they will see themselves as queens, go gaga over the bucolic spectacle, and, at night, indulge my every last whim. I'll be able to conduct myself like a satrap, enacting laws custom-made for me so that I can have the pleasure of breaking them tomorrow, forcing the peasants to wear shoes when they walk in the streets, or altering the number and times of the daily prayers."

Following Omar El Mabrouk, the gendarmes set up shop, then the police, then the officers of the military sector, then the Party bigwigs, the school teachers, the doctors and nurses at the hospital, the prison guards, the imam of the new mosque, the cashiers at the supermarket.

Ali son of Ali emigrated to the apartment over the new post office. He got his telephone and his numbered windows. Since he now oversaw a huge staff, he had no time to write our letters. The new mailman, a leper, refused to deliver our mail because we had no addresses.

"I need the name of the street and the number of the house."

We received no more news or money orders from our exiled sons in France.

Ultimately, Mohamed could not become mayor again.

Omar El Mabrouk preferred the former mayor of Sidi Bounemeur.

"His sole advantage is that he wasn't born among you."

The man staffed the town hall with young compatriots who received us haughtily and asked us for proof of residence.

"Our ancestors settled in this place a century and a half ago."

"I need an electric bill or a telephone bill."

One after another, our children went off and settled in the new city. At first, we saw a lot of them, but then their visits rapidly grew further and further apart. We had to sell off our goats, because we had no one to take care of them. This gave us some means of subsistence. But money eventually ran out. Our sons pretended not to know that we were needy. In fact, even though they themselves earned salaries, they never stopped complaining about the high cost of living and about the unreasonable demands of their children who were attending the government school: they wanted new shoes and clothes, lots of notebooks, and money to buy tidbits just like the children of the civilized people.

As in the old days, a few villagers went hungry. Yet they had to deny themselves, while the sacks of flour piled up at the supermarket.

We had been raised in dignified poverty, and those who had nothing to eat made it a point of honor to hide their destitution. Luckily, the son of Djelloul was on the alert. After his release from prison, the young man gave up his slingshot and devoted himself to reselling scarce items that he acquired underhandedly at the supermarket.

"All we have to do is buy and stock up," he assured us.

Since Djelloul was dead, his heart broken by his inactivity when he failed to convert to the blowtorch, his son transformed the inherited smithy into a store.

His booming business quickly consolidated his fortune. But he did not try to put up a lofty mansion or move to the new city. He generously supplied us with those products whose appearance on the supermarket shelves drew a stampede of customers; being old, we would have been trampled to death. We couldn't understand why all the merchandise was nowhere to be found.

"Have salaries made people's stomachs insatiable?"

The son of Djelloul would never accept a sou from us.

"I make up for it with the others. It's probably my bad conscience."

Omar El Mabrouk summoned the police commissioner the instant he arrived.

"I'm counting on you," he told him, "to establish law and order. Don't trust the villagers. They're sneaky and evil-minded. Don't be afraid to be harsh. I advise you to start by getting rid of all the young men who are just loafing around. They refuse to work in construction and they spend their days ogling the butts of the supermarket cashiers."

"What should we do with them?"

"The prison warden doesn't know what to do with his staff, so he'll be delighted to welcome those loafers."

"How can we justify arresting them?"

"You'll hit on something. That's your job."

The police began hunting down the insubordinate adolescents. The first were picked up for vagrancy.

"You have no employment or known source of income."

The next ones joined them because of illegal absenteeism.

"You hang around in the streets during the working hours of a workday. You ought to be at your jobs. You are thus absent without leave, since you have no authorization duly signed and sealed by your superior."

The last ones were jailed for crossing the new streets outside the marked pedestrian crossings.

The Party bigwig was welcomed by Omar El Mabrouk.

"A great deal of work is awaiting you here," he assured him. "The flock in this village has never been taken in hand."

For each block of apartment buildings, the Party appointed a warden to organize the distribution of water, the switching-off of lights, the days of voluntary service, the commemoration of legal holidays, and the convictions of the tenants. One day, a circular was pasted on all the doors of new buildings: it officially set the beginning of the month of Ramadan, which was one day later than the crescent moon that had been observed by all of us, myself included, and I can vouch for it even though I'm near-sighted. A learned personage forayed into the apparatuses that make you laugh and cry and he affirmed categorically that we could not have glimpsed a heavenly body that had not yet appeared. Nevertheless, a few troubled inhabitants of the new city came surreptitiously to consult our imam, who declared, "When you decided to leave us, we warned you that you were on the wrong track. You paid us no heed. Today, we tell you that our tired eyes may have deceived us. We are certain of nothing. Only Allah knows the truth. But he will not punish us for fasting one day earlier."

"They've guaranteed that their calculations are correct, and that no deviation has been ascertained since the creation of the world."

"You are free to follow the directives of those men who have become arrogant because they think they have mastered the knowledge of the Roumis. As for us, we will continue to obey the precepts of the Messenger."

"What should we do?"

"We warned you that if you left, you would condemn yourselves to living in chaos."

Torn to and fro, most of them decided to begin fasting on the same day as we did. When Omar El Mabrouk was alerted, he flew into a wild rage.

"That's sedition!"

He picked up his telephone to rant and rail at the Party bigwig.

"I warned you that the minds of these peasants are infested with more superstitions than my balls have crabs. It was your job to watch over their ideological and moral health."

Omar El Mabrouk dispatched squadrons of policemen into the streets and they forced the smokers to smoke, the tobacco-chewers to chew tobacco, those who weren't thirsty to drink, and those who weren't hungry to eat.

We again saw the teacher who had once come to open a school. Having been promoted to principal, he had no trouble seeing eye to eye with Omar El Mabrouk.

"Don't worry about the sons of the people who sent you packing. They deserve to be left to their dismal fate. And don't worry about the children of the civilized people. They're already in school. You'll be in charge of the offspring of the lepers and the people who have rallied to our cause."

The borehole drilled to furnish water to the city caused our own spring to run dry. Our sudden rage flushed Omar El Mabrouk out of his lair. He strode toward us followed by an army of policemen.

"I had no choice," he stated. "There's a shortage of water

in this country, you're well aware of that. It was a question of priority: you or your emigrated sons. They have their number and their future on their side."

Many of us died that year. I have already told you about Djelloul the blacksmith. The imam also died; he had been inconsolable since the loss of his power monopoly. Yet the foursome of the faithful that we were assured him that the new mosque was too far away for our old muscles, that we would continue to frequent the tiny room that had welcomed our earliest devotions, and that we preferred his sometimes obscure and often approximate sermons to the glittering rhetoric of his rival.

"He never stumbles over a verse, but his words are as hollow as a sheathe without a blade."

The rival helped to disrupt his colleague's discourse by switching on full blast the double pair of loudspeakers that provided ears for the minarets of the haughty temple. Even from a distance, his thundering logorrhea drowned out the old man's murmurs. Eventually, our imam gave up everything—preaching and praying, the illegal meetings of the djemaa—and sought refuge in reading the Holy Book. One day, they found the imam lying on his mat, the tome with the blackish-brown pages resting on his heart. He was dead. The Prophet himself died. Only God is immortal.

The imam had no successor. From then on, we prayed in disorder.

Many others left us in the course of that year. The guests of the fig-tree square were thinned out.

For lack of able-bodied men, our lands remained fallow and our olive trees neglected. There was no one left to take care of them but Moussa the son of Aïssa. After his father's disastrous funeral, the young man spent days on end vituperating non-step against Omar El Mabrouk; accusing him of causing the cripple's death. The young man threatened to kill the prefect. Aching for the paternal rifle that had been handed over to the foreigners, he armed himself with a knife and was about to march on the prefecture. It took our every last ounce of strength to stop him.

"The policemen guarding the entrance will never let you through. You'll be tossed in prison like so many of our adolescents."

Moussa the son of Aïssa then locked himself in the oil mill day and night, refusing to come out. He ate and prayed at the side of his machine.

Our insistent appeals managed only to get him to crack the door. He than vehemently ranted and railed at us.

"Stop wasting my time and go tend your olive trees. I'm repairing my press now. I'll soon have it working again. Hurry up and harvest your olives."

THERE WE ARE, I've finished my tale. You know the aftermath better than I do, for you were one of the leading figures in it. But since they neglected to teach you the language of your ancestors, I will speak to this machine for you.

"Who is that asshole?" Omar El Mabrouk asked his secretary.

We lived forgotten on the outskirts of the new village. On a day like any other day, the little lawyer came to visit us. He was in a jubilant mood, which clashed with our gloomy resignation.

"My son is coming in a few days," he told us.

We politely congratulated him without manifesting the slightest astonishment, whereas actually we hadn't even realized he was married.

"He's your son too in a way," he added in a slightly conspiratorial tone.

He explained that he had raised him in the religion of law and had succeeded in making him a judge.

"I even got him assigned to Zitouna. It wasn't hard: there wasn't exactly a mob of candidates. You'll see, lots of things are going to change around here."

We pointed out that it was precisely the upheavals that were the cause of our sufferings.

"The coming upheavals will be beneficial to you."

We shrugged our shoulders, convinced that for us, nothing could change.

"It's too late. We are nothing but survivors."

We added that we tended to distrust men of the law.

"Whenever we've appeared before them, all we've experienced is their unappealable fines."

"We have to believe in justice."

"Our experience has taught us that justice serves the powerful."

"That's not true. Justice serves law and equity."

"You yourself explained to us that you were exiled despite the law because you had dared to defend the weak and the helpless."

"Mine is a slightly special case."

"In any event, it's not injustice that we're suffering from today. Unless it's the kind that condemns us to being obsolete. But there's nothing your judge can do about that."

"At least he can protect you against being exploited by Omar El Mabrouk."

Our skeptical smiles, verging on impoliteness, hinted at our incredulity.

"This judge must be as small and fragile as you, since he's your son: would he dare to confront the powerful Omar El Mabrouk?"

"He's bigger and stronger than you imagine."

The lawyer insisted on introducing him to us as soon as he arrived.

Upon meeting him, we saw that the young man did not speak our language. So we used the tongue of the Koran.

The son of the little lawyer was the spit and image of the civilized inhabitants of the villa development. But we were astonished at his size. He was almost as immense as Omar El Mabrouk. We insisted they stay for dinner. Since we had no animal to slaughter, the son of Djelloul had to go to the butcher shop and buy some quarters of sheep. The couscous tasted insipid. We could not, in all fairness, blame the inexperience or negligence of our women. We had to conclude that the blandness of our favorite dish was due to an inadequate performance of the ritual sacrifice.

"It's simply the bleakness of the days that we are living. Those who have departed must be less unhappy."

This remark filled our evening with a nostalgic bitterness. The enthusiasm and loquacity of the father had no effect on the reserve of the young man, who remained taciturn if not circumspect. He must have learned to distrust the lawyer's untimely initiatives.

"He's listening to you. Go ahead, speak," the little man insisted.

We explained to him that we had nothing left to hope for and that we would rather he devoted his efforts to defending the rights of our sons who had been thoughtless enough to emigrate to the new city.

"We have chosen our fate and we are bowing to it. Our grandchildren have denied us and have opted for a different way. Between the two, our sons are going to live in disorder and heartbreak. They are the most miserable."

"He's here to listen to you," the lawyer repeated. "Go ahead and speak."

After several gestures of reluctance, the son of Djelloul the blacksmith talked about Moussa, who had been locked up in his press for several months.

"Why has he done that?" the judge asked.

His father briefly outlined the case in the language of the Roumis.

"That edict is unjust and illegal," the magistrate concluded. "It can be quashed."

"What good would that do?" the old lawyer asked vehemently. "That donkey press dates back to Moussa's grandfather. Its gears are more arthritic than my joints. It can never start working again. Not to mention that your neglected trees produce nothing but sickly olives with more bone than flesh; no one wants to harvest them just as no one wants to consume their unrefined oil with its burning taste."

"The Koran itself," I told him, "recommends olive oil. It's a medicament that heals our bodies of so many ailments."

"The closing of the press caused Aïssa to die; and his heir may suffer the same fate," added the son of Djelloul. "I'm sure that Moussa will come out of his lair once he is free to let the gears of his machine start grinding again. Who cares if the mill produces anything. Let *him* decide whether or not to stop it. Let him decide if there's a reason to wreck his problematic legacy. The mill is old, but Moussa is young."

"We risk fighting for a cause that's lost in advance," the little lawyer objected.

"Aren't you the one who was called the obdurate defender of lost causes?"

The judge stood up, apparently unaware of his rudeness.

"It is time to confront Omar El Mabrouk," he announced.

"You don't know Omar El Mabrouk," I retorted. "He's a strong and powerful man, and his anger is terrible, whereas you don't even have a moustache."

"Remember the example of the mountebank's kestrel: victory often belongs to the more resolute. I have an old score to settle with that man."

* * *

"Who is that asshole?"

Stooped from fearful submission, the secretary tried to calm the grumbling of Omar El Mabrouk.

"He's the judge."

"I'm quite aware of that, you moron. But what else? What's his family background? Which clan does he belong to? Who's the strong man who protects him? He must enjoy some powerful support if he dares to defy me like this. Is this some new plot hatched up by my enemies? Isn't it enough for them to have exiled me here?"

"Supposedly, he's the son of the little lawyer."

"Really? But that little lawyer is nothing. When did the judge arrive?"

"About a month ago."

"Why wasn't I warned?"

"I told you about him. You didn't feel it was useful to receive him."

"I should have. If I'd explained the situation, I could have prevented him from committing such blunders. He really quashed my edict? Does he want to annoy me or what? Doesn't he know who I am? His father should've warned him. Send out two cops pronto and tell them to bring him back in handcuffs. I'll teach him which side his bread is buttered on."

Half an hour later, the secretary returned to Omar El Mabrouk's office.

"Where is he?"

"He refuses to come."

"What do you mean?? Do those stupid policemen think they got their six-shooters just so they can dazzle the floozies at the supermarket? Couldn't they stick their guns into that showoff's ribs?"

"He's a magistrate."

"How often do I have to tell you that the only magistrate

here is me! That guy obviously hasn't caught on that the only reason he's here is to force these shitfaces to cough up their taxes; and to settle conflicts between the citified peasant women. All he has to do is hand down stiff sentences to the delinquents that the police bring him. Why is he attacking me? Does he have a grudge against me or what? Did his father sick him on me? That guy could have remained minister if he hadn't acted like such an asshole. He's a dangerous man. I'm going to send him to the top of the mountain, where he can live in my grandfather Hassan's shanty. He can instruct the foxes and boars about their rights. I know that the press is useless and that the inhabitants at the middle-income projects have learned to prefer the clear, tasteless oil that's sold at the supermarket. This makes it all the more serious. His decision is an act of defiance. If I don't react, he'll be encouraged by the precedent. That greenhorn is going to learn who he's dealing with. His ridiculous robe won't shield him from my temper."

Omar El Mabrouk leaped up so violently from his seat that he knocked over his desk. Three strides brought him to the door, and his shoulders banged the leaves as he passed through. He dashed into the corridor, panicking the clerks, who slipped out any possible exits or hugged the walls to let the cyclone pass. Omar El Mabrouk came out on the steps in front of the prefecture, scattering the two sentries from the breast summer, and strode toward the tribunal. Disrupting everyone he passed, he juggernauted across the courtroom, inspected the offices, then, at a terrified sign from the janitor, he climbed up to the judge's chambers on the next floor.

The prefect's violent intrusion did not faze the two men who were there.

The judge stood up to receive the august visitor.

The two men stared at each other for a long time.

The little lawyer told us that at the end of that gambit, Omar El Mabrouk suddenly calmed down, as if under a spell, and even docilely agreed to take the seat indicated by his antagonist. He was probably disconcerted by meeting a man who could return his stare.

"I was waiting for you," his host said.

The little lawyer watched the scene jubilantly.

"What's this all about?" the prefect asked.

"You had absolutely no legal grounds for shutting down the mill. I have therefore decided in favor of the plaintiff."

"I don't give a good goddamn about this business of the olive-grinding machine. And I'm sure you don't either. You wanted to provoke me."

"I'm here to render justice."

"Fuck your justice. Who got you into the university, who let you squeeze your ass against the asses of those pretty coeds while you pretended to be engrossed in studying articles of those complex and futile legal codes? If me and my buddies hadn't taken up arms to liberate you, you'd still be cleaning the dung off your clodhoppers. Don't forget who you owe your judge's robe to."

"Did you rise up against the colonizer in order to replace him?"

"Have we met before?"

"No, never."

"Who are you?"

"A man who is simply doing his job."

"Has your father incited you against me?"

"No, not at all."

"Then who sent you?"

"An old mountain bandit: Hassan El Mabrouk."

"My grandfather? He's been dead for years."

"Probably."

"Then what's this all about?"

The judge stood up and took down the rifle hanging on the wall. He offered it to the prefect, who clutched it mechanically.

"This man who is with us here is not my real father?"

"Then who are you?"

"The heir to the weapon. Do you recognize it?"

"No."

"This is Hassan El Mabrouk's rifle. I must warn you that it's loaded. So stop squeezing it."

The little lawyer spoke up for the first time.

"It was I who took the rifle that Hassan El Mabrouk left behind when he invaded the lieutenant's villa, just as I took the son of Ourida who had died in childbirth. Your sister Ourida."

"You're out of your gourd. I have no sister. I never had a sister. Ourida never existed. That rutting bitch who threw herself into the lieutenant's arms was not my sister."

"You ought to respect your sister's memory," the little man went on, "for she was worth more than you. I knew her very well, you see. And you must have an inkling of how tragically she suffered. It's your remorse that's made you deny her very existence. And perhaps you've really managed to erase her from your mind and thereby wipe out the memory of your abuse. Remember what happened between the two of you after she came to yank you from the arms of Suzanne, the daughter of Martial. And so many other nights. You're the rutting dog. She was already pregnant when you joined the underground. She wanted to protect you by avoiding any scandal. She begged the lieutenant to keep her in the villa. He agreed to hire her as a cleaning woman. But he fell in love with her. He offered to marry her and adopt her child. She refused, afraid of abjuring her faith by marrying a non-Moslem. The poor woman went through a martyrdom. We made a pact with the officer to keep the birth a secret. Whether the child was yours or his, it would have lived the life of an outcast."

After a moment of silence, the lawyer stood up.

"I'm leaving. This is something that has to be settled between the two of you. I gave the rifle to your son, and he has just returned it to you. So it's up to you to decide. You can point the barrel at the judge, squeeze the trigger, and there will be no one to oppose you. But you have another possibility."

Omar El Mabrouk leaped up from his chair.

"That man is not my son, he's the bastard brat of the lieutenant and that slut Ourida!"

We were told that Omar El Mabrouk dashed away, taking along the rifle. He placed a dozen policemen around his residence to defend it, and he locked himself up inside.

Some people claim he's killed himself, but no one knows for sure. You are his son, I think you ought to go and see.

That's that: with the help of Allah, my story is finished. You can switch off the machine.

It is beginning to get dark in this prayer room. Come, let's go out and stroll a bit. Look, the sun is setting. If you knew my language, you would have certainly asked me to show you the fig-tree square. There it is, in front of us. The trees are gone. A strange disease devoured the bases of their trunks, and one very windy day, they toppled over, still embracing like eternal lovers. Our life here had the same solidarity. The roots are still alive. Look at the young shoots that are taking. Will they survive?

If you can help me, I'll walk a bit in the fields and smell the fragrance of the grass. This tale has aroused the memories of my youth. . . . It was long ago. . . . Very long ago. . . . I believe I feel like dying.

ABOUT THE AUTHOR

Rachid Mimouni was born on November 20, 1945 at Bou-douaou (Alma), thirty kilometers east of Algiers, into a family of poor peasants. He received his primary education in Boudouaou, his secondary education in Rouiba, and his higher education in Algiers (with a degree in science in 1968). As a research assistant at the Institute of Industrial Development, he completed his education with two years of study in Montreal. He currently teaches at the National Institute of Production and Industrial Development. In Algeria, he published *Le Printemps n'en sera que plus beau* (*The Spring Will Only Be More Beautiful*), in 1978, *Une Peine à vivre* (*The Trouble with Living*), in 1984, *Tombéza,* also in 1984, and *La Ceinture de l'ogresse* (*The Belt of the Ogress*), in 1990. *Le Fleuve détourné* (*The Diverted River*), his first novel published in France, in 1982, received exceptional reviews.